"Carrick?"

I lean forward and put my head against his. Our hearts are beating exactly in tandem. I can feel mine, and his, too. It's weird but also oddly satisfying.

His arms come off the table and around my waist. He holds me as if I'm all that is standing between him and hell, and maybe I am. I pull him closer and wait for him to say something.

"You can't help me, you know," he says. "This isn't about some magic or some gift."

He desires me, but it's against his will. And he won't do anything about it. He pulls away and stands up, his head averted. The smell of him stays in my nostrils.

It will never go away.

Kate Austin

Kate Austin has worked as a legal assistant, a commercial fisher, a brewery manager, a teacher, a technical writer and a herring popper, while managing to read an average of a book a day. Go ahead—ask her anything. If she doesn't know the answer she'll make it up, because she's been reading and writing fiction for as long as she can remember.

She blames her mother and her two grandmothers for her reading-and-writing obsession—all of them were avid readers and they passed the books and the obsession on to her. She lives in Vancouver, Canada, where she can walk on the beach whenever necessary, even in the rain.

She'd be delighted to hear from readers through her Web site, www.kateaustin.ca.

SEEING IS BELIEVING

Kate Austin

SEEING IS BELIEVING

copyright © 2007 by Kate Austin

isbn-13:978-0-373-88144-4

isbn-10:   0-373-88144-4

This is a work of fiction. Names, characters, places and incidents are
either the product of the author's imagination or are used fictitiously,
and any resemblance to actual persons, living or dead, business
establishments, events or locales is entirely coincidental.

This edition published by arrangement with Harlequin Books S.A.

® and TM are trademarks of the publisher. Trademarks indicated with
® are registered in the United States Patent and Trademark Office, the
Canadian Trade Marks Office and in other countries.

TheNextNovel.com

 HARLEQUIN®

PRINTED IN U.S.A.

From the Author

Dear Reader,

We live in a magical world—and you see it everywhere as soon as you start looking for it. There's magic in the quarter moon shining on a perfect spring night. There's magic in the ducklings paddling in the pond out back. There's magic in a baby's kiss and, more than anything else, there's magic in love.

Ria Sterling has her fair share of magic but she's not at all sure she wants it, and she's certain she's not ready for it. Whether she's ready for it or not, she can't help but believe in something that's so much a part of her life. Carrick Jones, on the other hand, doesn't believe in magic of any kind. Detective Jones believes in the power of logic.

Put the two of them together and what do you get? You guessed it. Magic.

I hope you'll enjoy Ria and Carrick as much as I did. Send me a note via my Web site, www.kateaustin.ca, and let me know what you think.

Kate

For Tara Gavin, who consistently and lovingly
makes me a better writer.

CHAPTER 1

"He's going to die."

I see his death in the photograph because that's what I do—it's my gift and like many gifts from the gods, it isn't a good one. I hate it. Especially on days such as today when some crying mother or wife or lover hands me a photograph and waits for me to tell her that she's right to be scared to death.

Because I can see it coming. Almost never in time to change it, but that doesn't stop them from showing up on my doorstep, eyes bright with unshed tears.

"I can't cry," they say. "Not until I know for sure."

"Please," they say. "Tell me what you see."

My gift from the gods is to see death.

James Foster. It's his death I see today and I know by the time his mother and sister get home their phone will be ringing and some jaded cop from a jurisdiction two or three time zones away will be breaking the news.

I don't know how he'll die, I only know he will. Soon. Probably before I finish turning off my computer and turning on the alarm system.

Some gift. Foresight, precognition, prescience. Doesn't matter what you call it, not really. It all boils down to the same thing.

People come to me as a last resort, asking a question to which they don't want the answer. When I was much younger, I thought I might figure out a way to avoid their pain. Lying, I thought, or silence. But they saw it in my face and over the years I discovered that the words seemed to make it easier on them. As my reputation grew, the words themselves took on power.

"He's going to die."

I never had to add that it would be soon. Anyone who knew how to find me knew that before they rang the doorbell.

I have tried, over and over, to strengthen my gift, to make it more useful, to see further into the future.

"It's a gift. You can't change it like a shirt that doesn't fit," my mother says, but she doesn't have to live with it.

I want to save someone, anyone. I want to be in time. But I have learned to stop wishing for the impossible. In the darkest hours of the night, I still want to stop the truck bearing down on them or the knife raised in anger.

But in thirty years and hundreds of photos, I have saved only two people. Or at least I choose to think I have. But perhaps my vision was wrong, skewed by the alignment of the stars or a head cold. Maybe that particular couple was not meant to die. Even including that couple in my save percentage only brings it up to less than one-tenth of one percent. Not enough to be statistically significant....

I was five and my mother had left a magazine on the kitchen table.

I looked at the man on the cover and I started to cry. My mother said later that I was inconsolable, that I wept right through the night. By the next morning, I couldn't see out my swollen eyes or breathe through my aching nose. I stopped crying when the noon news came on the radio.

"Elvis Presley has died," the announcer said. "Last night, at his home in Memphis, the King passed away."

My tears stopped as my mother began to cry.

After the death of the King, I lived a normal life—not even realizing what was missing in our house. Photographs. And the lack of them wasn't about me. None of us had figured it out then; my crying was simply a fluke. We just weren't a family for photographs.

I was a baby when my photographer father left with the cameras.

"So what?" my mother said. "Who needs photos? I have you. All I have to do is look up and there you are." She'd grab my cheeks and smile at me.

Photos weren't a part of my childhood. I don't think my mother had a photograph of my father, not even a wedding shot. I knew what he looked like because of the mirror in the bathroom.

"You look just like him," my mother would sigh. She'd touch my nose, my cheeks, my lips. "Poor child, you look just like him."

I never felt deprived. Whenever I needed my father's advice, I went to the mirror and asked him. Sometimes the answer didn't come right away, or didn't make sense, or it took me months to figure out what question the answer was for, but there was always an answer.

I remember being glad I didn't have to see him to know him—he was always there for me. He was a good man, with strong clean features. His nose was straight, his cheekbones obvious, his eyes changing from olive green to brown depending on the light. His hair was a mousy colour, lightening with streaks of gold and red in the summer. I knew he was handsome because that's what my Aunt Lucy told me.

"You'll never be pretty, girl, but you'll be handsome. Boys won't get it, but men will. So don't fret, you'll come into your own just when all those Barbie dolls are losing it. You'll be fine."

I believed her.

I DON'T KNOW HOW PEOPLE find out about me. They never tell, and I don't ask. I keep a very low profile, no advertising (what would I say? Deaths predicted, loved ones lost?), no interviews, no money. I do it because I have to.

It wasn't always this way. For many years, the gift lurked only in nightmares. I was thirteen before it happened again and this time it scared the hell out of all of us.

We were in a pizza parlour—our regular Friday night treat. It was Gran's turn to pick the songs on the jukebox so she wandered over and stood there, hands on her hips, staring at the numbers. We knew she couldn't see them and that eventually she'd press buttons at random. The results could be anything from "What's Love Got to Do With It?" to "Careless Whispers." That night it was "Money for Nothing."

Aunt Lucy and Mom swapped stories while I sat,

head in hands, dreaming about the new boy in my math class. The woman at the next table—red hair, bright yellow scarf wrapped around it—pulled a magazine from her bag. I wasn't really looking at her or the magazine, but one glance was enough. The man on the front cover vanished in a storm of tears.

"Ria, honey, what's wrong?"

Sobs caught in my throat. I couldn't speak.

"Ria, come on, sweetie, tell us what's wrong."

No words, only sobs. They gathered me up and took me home and I cried all night. Inconsolable yet again, and no one knew why. But this time we figured out that the crying was triggered by the photo on the magazine, and this time we figured out why it stopped.

"Rock Hudson died," Gran said in a voice shaking with unshed tears. "He died of that plague thing."

The moment his name left her lips, the tears stopped. I hiccupped for a few minutes.

"Rock Hudson? I saw his picture last night… It made me cry."

FROM THEN ON I AVOIDED photos. The TV didn't do it, nor movies, and I was safe at school. History books were full of already-dead people. We didn't get a newspaper or magazines and I never looked at catalogues.

A year passed and I began to feel safe. But of course I wasn't.

I caught a glimpse of a photograph for the year-book, not close enough to identify the people in it, but enough for my gift to kick in. I knew these kids, had seen them in the hallways, had classes with one girl's younger sister.

I went to bed and stayed there for a month. My mother had no difficulty convincing the doctor I was sick—after crying non-stop for a week I looked like a victim of a disaster. Flood. Fire. Famine. I'd fit in anywhere there were thousands lying injured or dead.

This time there was no relief. The hours of reporting on TV and radio didn't stop the tears, nor did my mother's chicken soup. I stood in the back of several different churches for the services where ministers spoke of God's will and I thought of the drunk drivers—one in their car, one in another—who'd killed them. That didn't help either.

I lost weight so fast that pretty soon I couldn't get out of bed. I'd try to eat but even soup choked me. The doctor wanted me fed intravenously but my mother refused to let me stay in the hospital.

Aunt Lucy, the only one who didn't fall apart every time she saw me, learned to administer the IV and stayed home while my mother and Gran worked.

No one knew what to do—not our family doctor, who'd known me since birth, not the psychiatrists or the child welfare workers. All they could say was, "She's a teenager, you have to expect mood swings."

I laugh at that now, but at the time it added a healthy dose of rage to my grief. It didn't stop the tears but I did get a little stronger. My weight loss slowed and I began to get a little sleep.

And then the miracle occurred.

CHAPTER 2

Friday night was now the one night all three of the women sat by my bed, pizza night having been swallowed up by circumstances outside our control. The TV had been moved up to my room, along with everyone's favorite chairs. We watched Don Johnson in *Miami Vice*, ate popcorn and drank sodas.

I learned to control the sobbing long enough to avoid choking on the popcorn husks. Aunt Lucy hooked up the intravenous for most of the week, but Friday nights we pretended I was getting better and she pulled it from my arm while I drank sodas and nibbled on pizza crusts and popcorn husks.

The doorbell rang.

"Is Dr. Cameron coming by tonight?" Mom looked at Aunt Lucy, who shrugged.

"I don't think so. He saw Ria on Wednesday. I don't know why he'd come back."

"Gran? Are you expecting someone?"

My grandmother, a bright, cheerful and still beautiful sixty-five, had more dates than the three of us put together. She shook her head.

"You know I don't go out on Friday nights."

The bell rang again.

"Just answer it," Aunt Lucy said. "It's probably a salesman."

Gran perked up. "I'll go."

We waited impatiently for her to clomp down the stairs and back up. Crockett and Tubbs would be on in a minute and if we had to fill Gran in, the show would be ruined.

Two voices drifted up the stairs but I couldn't distinguish any words or even the gender of the second voice. Mom, Aunt Lucy and I sat silently, the commercials playing like music in the background, our ears open to any hints from below.

"Joan? Lucy? Come down here for a minute."

Mom and Aunt Lucy looked at each other. I saw the "huh?" in their eyes but they followed Gran downstairs.

Now I was curious.

Fifteen minutes passed. I finished the popcorn but couldn't focus on the unfolding story. Who could take my family away from my bedside on a Friday night? I was tempted by the stairs, but I hadn't been further from my bed than the bathroom next door in a month and wasn't sure my legs would hold me on the excursion.

Crockett almost got killed, Tubbs rescued him, together they captured the bad guy and I still waited.

Mom came back up the stairs just as the closing credits rolled. Good thing, because that hour's box of tissue was almost gone and I hated getting my pajamas wet.

"Ria, honey, you have a visitor." Her voice was carefully uninflected as she reached over and turned off the television.

"Who is it? I don't want to see anybody, Mom. Not like this."

I gestured down at myself, at the bones poking out from my wrists, and the basket overflowing with tissues.

"Look at me," I wept, "no one can see this face."

Mom wouldn't even let me see it. The mirrors in my bedroom and the bathroom had been removed, the curtains stayed closed, ostensibly because the light hurt my eyes (and it did), but even more so I couldn't see my reflection in the window at night.

"You have to see her, and she won't care about how you look."

"No."

Both of us knew the tantrum was coming but this time, I chose not to stop it.

"No. No. No. I'm not seeing anybody." My voice got louder until I was screaming through the tears. "No. Get out of my room."

The tissue box sailed across the room and hit the wall behind my mother. I reached for the empty pop bottle as she stepped out and slammed the door behind her.

"I won," I whispered, my hands shaking. "I won."

The room settled into silence around me. I felt the tears on my face, soothing the rage I knew disfigured it. I didn't want the gift, didn't want to be a freak. I wanted to move to another place—one without cameras—and start my life over. But even if we moved, nothing would change. Nothing. Not ever. I stoked my anger, repeating, "I won. I won," to the empty room.

"No, my angel, you did not win anything at all."

A tiny figure had stepped into the room, a halo of light surrounding her. I blinked, shedding more tears, trying to dispel the illusion. I looked up, my eyes temporarily clear. The figure remained. The room was bathed in a warm, clear light and, though I wanted to deny it, the light came from the woman at the foot of my bed.

"Ria." She rolled the R of my name, turning it into four or five syllables. "Look at me, child."

My head came up of its own volition and I focused on her face, on my face in miniature. I took a deep breath, and another, but still couldn't speak. I wanted to ask…

"Who I am? You want to know who I am and why your mother and grandmother and your Aunt Lucy allowed me into your house and your room. You want to know why you feel as if you recognize me when you know you have never seen me before."

I nodded, both in confirmation and encouragement.

"I will make everything clear, my angel, but first… First you need to stop crying."

"I c-c-c-can't," I said through my hiccups. "I can't."

"Of course you can. You managed to stop the last time, did you not?"

"But I don't know why. Or how."

"I do not expect you to know these things now, Ria. You are only embarking on this journey, not completing it. Come, my child," she reached out her hand to me, "it is time for you to get out of your bed."

THE SUN SHINES INTO the deepest recesses of the porch, illuminating even the darkest corners. The spiders have been busy during the week, spinning webs and catching flies. I smile, a little sad at this evidence of Gran's failing health. Even a year ago those spiders wouldn't have stood a chance.

The broom feels light in my hands—hands more accustomed to wielding a welding torch than any type of cleaning tool. Despite this, the old hickory shaft, smoothed by years of spider bashing, conveys a sense of order, of home and warmth and comfort. I look up at the webs once more and sit down on the swing, the spiders safe for this night.

Mama Amata brought the broom with her when she arrived that Friday night just over twenty years ago and saved my life. She left it behind when she disappeared again. We've been using it ever since.

Mom has often asked me if I wanted to take the broom to my house. But it felt right for it to be here. This house is my refuge and the broom serves to remind me of how lucky I am to be alive and to have such a place. I believe, all three of us believe, that without Mama Amata I would have died in the summer of 1985.

I would have cried until not a single drop of moisture remained in my body, sucked dry like a fly caught in a spider's web. I would have gradually lightened until I collapsed in on myself, desiccated and dead.

I hear the women of my family in the kitchen. Gran is almost totally deaf now so the volume is more than loud enough to make out the words even here at the other end of the house.

"I'll make the dressing," my mother yells.

"It's already made. I did it on Wednesday." Gran's voice, wavering but more than clear enough to penetrate the brick walls between us.

I don't have to hear the next part of the conversation. Mom is surreptitiously making new dressing to replace the rancid one made three days ago while Aunt Lucy distracts Gran, pulling the bread from the oven, handing her the cutlery and the plates.

Dinner is soon safely on the table and, as we do every Friday evening, we begin the meal by thanking Mama Amata that the four of us are still together and that I have learned to live with my gift, rather than allowing it to kill me.

For the first time in months I spend the weekend in peace: no calls, no work, no death. When I return home and open the front door on Sunday night, even my dark house seems to welcome me with a comfortable blanket of silence. I take a quick glance into the office, enjoying the lack of flashing lights—

neither the computer nor the answering machine blinks at me.

I'm not sure what to do with myself. I've had two days without death and, although I try to push the thought away, I can't help but wonder if I'm missing it, if death has become my lifeline.

I sit in the kitchen, a glass of wine in my hand and try to ignore the voice in my head. "Nice try, Ria," I whisper. Have I learned to crave the power?

The fridge hums, the red light of the clock on the microwave faintly warms the darkness. I can't turn on the lights, can't even open the fridge for another glass of wine. I'm not ready to see my reflection in the window.

I've felt this despair coming on for months, but I've been ignoring it. If I allow it in, I believe I will somehow dishonor my gift and my ancestors. But now, sitting in this dark silence, bolstered by a weekend without pain, I can't deny the temptation.

It's not that I miss the death, it's that I want to walk away from the faces that haunt me.

I shake my head and finish the wine. I've been here before. There have been many times when the despair threatened to overwhelm me. The bottle of wine in the fridge beckons—release from the thoughts roiling about in my head—but so does the

morning. Six o'clock comes early and no one but a
fool does my job without all of their senses clear.

Welding torches do not forgive mistakes.

THE WEEK PASSES AND SO, at least for a time, does my
despair. The gods have granted me a much-needed
respite and I enjoy it without anticipating its inevitable end.

"There will be times, my angel, when you will feel
as if you cannot go on, when you wish to abandon
your gift. At those times, the gods often grant you
time for reflection."

Mama Amata's voice echoes in my head as I work
in the yard; her face appears on the computer screen
as I clean up my files. She told me many things that
night and although I don't remember all of them, her
voice comes to me at times like this.

It's as if she programmed the computer in my
head, setting it to buzz a reminder when needed. I
don't remember ever hearing these particular voices
before, but they are clear and loud now.

The family leaves me alone. They've learned my
moods aren't improved by food or movies or gossip,
only by time. They know I'll call them when I'm ready.

I work myself out of my distraction and by Friday
I'm ready to get back to the work I need to be

doing. After a shower, a scotch, and a good night's sleep, that is.

I walk in the door, reeking of sweat and dirt and aching in every muscle. It's been a bitch of a week. A miserable job, a miserable boss and miserable weather. It's been pouring down rain all week and I already have five pairs of jeans and shirts growing mold in the laundry room.

I rip off my filthy clothes and race up the stairs.

"A shower, a scotch, and dinner with the family. I can't think of anything better, can you, Fatcat?" He hisses as I drop my sodden T-shirt on his head.

Fatcat showed up on my back porch last week, just when I needed him. Now he won't leave. But he won't purr either, or be cuddled. He slashes at my ankles when I walk by, pounces at me when I'm sitting down, and orders his food with all the arrogance of a prince. I love him. Maybe because it's so obvious he doesn't give a damn about me. For Fatcat, it's all about the food.

The shower pounds away a portion of the grime but rids me of none of the anxiety I've been feeling since noon. Something is coming. Someone. I mean someone is coming. Soon.

CHAPTER 3

When the doorbell rings, I'm sitting in my office, hands on my lap, ready for whoever it is. I have called my mother to tell her I won't be home for dinner. I reassure her that I'm fine, that I'm not depressed, that it's work, not despair.

I have paid my bills and arranged for a gardener to water and cut the grass.

I don't know how I know to do these things. I have known since noon that I must get organized because… Because why? I have never before anticipated something or someone's arrival. I'm still as surprised by the arrival of my nine hundred and ninety-ninth client as I was by the first. That's why I have the answering service, the cell phone, the pager, because I don't know when someone will show up.

I will have to work (I'm in the middle of a job and can't walk out on them) but I have cancelled everything else. Or if it can't be cancelled—like Fatcat and the lawn—I have arranged for them to be dealt with by someone other than me.

I don't know what to expect, but I'm ready.

There are two men at my door, one tall and broad, the other as close as can be to average without being a caricature of it.

"Ms. Sterling?" the tall one asks. "I'm Detective Jones." He holds out his ID and I see it before I realize I should turn away. But I notice only two things: his first name is Carrick and he doesn't look at all like his photograph.

"This is Detective Morrison," Jones gestures at Mr. Average.

Morrison holds out his photograph. This time, I try to turn my head away but it's too late.

I have learned to conquer the rush of tears and nausea which comes with the gift but the strength of the feeling always takes my breath away.

"Ms. Sterling?" Carrick Jones lightly touches my shoulder. "Are you all right?"

I shrug away from him. Cops are both incredibly perceptive and blind at one and the same time. They know you're lying—for them, everyone is always lying—but not why. Good.

"I'm fine."

I lead them into the office even though it's almost

too small for the three of us. I don't want Morrison in my living space.

"Come in and tell me what you want."

I motion at the two chairs in front of my desk and I sit, safe behind three feet of IKEA plasterboard.

They wait, politely, for me to get comfortable before sitting down, their elbows bumping the walls and each other. They take over my space and make it their own. I'd like to learn that trick. It would come in handy on certain jobs, with certain foremen.

The sound of breathing fills up the room until I feel as if I might drown in it. My fingers tighten around the pen I've picked up to help keep my eyes averted from Morrison. I've never before met someone I knew would die, and I'm scared. Not just because I'm sitting across the desk from a dead man, but because I'm panicking about the how of it.

Any moment—a bomb, a plane crashing into my roof, Jones going ballistic and shooting both of us, a fire or a tornado. Whatever is going to kill Morrison has a good chance of taking me, too.

I know it won't take Jones—I saw his photograph and he's safe—but I don't know about me.

I force myself to sit quietly and wait. The authorities will not like me. Anyone who predicts death must be suspect in some way. So I wait, inwardly in turmoil, outwardly calm. I will *not* speak first.

The silence stretches until I am within a single moment of breaking it. I open my mouth to speak, but Jones beats me to it.

"You are Ria Sterling, aren't you?"

I wonder if he wants to see some identification or if I am not what he expects. A crone? A gypsy? Someone older or younger?

"Yes," I say.

Another thing I've learned from television. Don't speak first and don't volunteer anything, not one word more than is required to answer the question.

"Do you recognize this woman?"

I flinch and close my eyes as he hands me a photograph, an automatic defence mechanism. I do not look at family photographs, I do not read magazines or newspapers, I do not own a camera or know a photographer. I have a complete set of defences against using the gift by accident. Yes, of course my life is circumscribed by them, but they work. At least most of the time.

One of the reasons (besides money) I work in construction is because men do not often want to show you the pictures of their vacation or their new grandson. They're happy to talk about last night's hockey game and they don't need to show you pictures of the big fight.

"Ms. Sterling, do you recognize this woman?" Detective Jones asks me again, impatience in his voice.

I hold the photograph gripped tightly in my hand but don't look. I hate cameras and I hate their product.

"Open your eyes."

The voice is gentle but it is an order, not a request. I refuse it.

"Do you know what I do?" I ask, my eyes squeezed shut. "Do you understand what you're asking?"

"Ms. Sterling, the rumor around the station is that you're some kind of a witch. Now, I know that's not true but the Chief wants us to talk to you. We've come across town to see you so we can say we've done it. Open your damn eyes. Now."

The anger in that heretofore calm voice jolts me into action but when I open my eyes I still avoid looking at the photograph.

"I'm not a witch."

"Well, we're desperate so I don't give a good goddamn if you're Mickey Mouse. Look at the photograph."

I can't do it, not with Morrison sitting there. I shake my head.

"Let me tell you what I do," I say, looking straight

across the desk and into eyes as blue as the waters of Crete. "If you still want me to look afterwards, I will."

Jones settles back into his chair with barely concealed impatience.

"Go ahead. Tell us."

"I see death," I begin, using words I've spoken a thousand times. "Somehow I see people's deaths in their photographs. It never works in person or on the television. It doesn't work if the person is already dead. It doesn't matter if I know them or if the photograph is fifty years older than the person in it. I look at a photograph and, if the person is going to die soon, and I mean really soon, I see it."

A snort signifies Jones' disgust. "You expect me to believe this shit?"

"I don't care if you believe it or not. You've come to me so somebody over there thinks it's worth a shot."

"Huh. Right along with the Psychic Friends Network. This is a waste of time." Jones lunges out of his chair but Morrison grabs his arm.

"We can't go back without showing her the picture. Just do it, okay?"

Jones shrugs his shoulders. I know they'll sit there until I look at their stupid photograph. Or maybe they'll take me to the station.

I brace myself for the shock and look down at the

picture in my hands. Nothing happens. I rub my thumb over the woman's face. She looks familiar and for a moment I think I must know her, but I don't. I have, though, seen her face on the news. She's missing. Her name is…

"Lisa Alison Martin. She's been missing for two days."

I hold up my hand.

"I know who she is. But the photo says nothing to me."

I don't say what this most probably means—that Lisa Alison Martin is already dead. Instead I say again, "Nothing. It means nothing to me."

"Of course it doesn't." The sarcasm drops from his mouth like acid. "Why would it? It's all a game to you, isn't it? Suckering all those poor schmucks who come to you for help, ripping them off while they're in pain.

"Come on, Morrison, let's get the hell out of here."

I scribble frantically on a piece of paper on my desk. I don't know why I want Carrick Jones to believe me but it's important. I put his name on an envelope and seal it.

"Take this. But don't open it until Monday."

I'm not sure whether he'll do what I ask nor what the cost of this action will be, but it's necessary. He takes the envelope and shoves it into his pocket.

"Thank you, Ms. Sterling, for nothing."

I take care not to touch Morrison as I follow the two of them to the door. Even without touch, a wave of sorrow rolls over me. I can't tell if it's him or me, but it's strong. I stumble and fall against him.

"Oh my God." I crumple to the floor, curling myself into a ball to get away from him. "Oh my God. Oh. Oh. Oh."

The agony is relentless, affecting every part of my body. My head throbs, my heart pounds.

"Call 9-1-1. Now."

I hear Carrick Jones through the haze of pain. And then everything and everyone vanishes.

CHAPTER 4

My head aches. The lights in the ceiling hurt my eyes and I can't see where I am.

"Mom? Gran? Aunt Lucy?"

No one answers. But I smell a faint aroma of life underneath the stench of disinfectant and pain. Someone is in the room with me. I blink, wait for my eyes to settle down enough to see through the glare, and take another deep breath. I recognize the smell, but I can't put a person to it.

The green walls are the first thing I see, then the railings on the bed. I'm in a hospital. Duh. Of course I am, the disinfectant should have given it away. A chair has been pulled up to the foot of the bed and I have to sit up to see who's in it. Obviously not a nurse, or any of my family, they'd be sitting right next to me.

"Detective Jones?"

The look on his face tells me. He's not here

because I fainted. He's here because his partner died and he wants to know how the hell I knew.

"He's dead, isn't he? Morrison's dead."

No response. He's scaring me.

"Jones? Come on, tell me what's happening."

I crawl out of the covers and down to the end of the bed. Before I can stop myself, I reach for his face. He flinches.

"Don't touch me," he whispers.

The stare and the angry whisper are more effective than a scream. Carrick Jones would kill me if he wasn't a cop. He might do it anyway. I back away until I feel the panic button under my hand. I pull it into my palm and put my thumb on the button.

"How did you do it?"

I have to strain to hear him. It's as if he's got a wad of cotton stuck halfway down his throat and he's speaking around it. I don't know how he can breathe through it.

"I told you. I told you yesterday."

"No. Not that."

"What then?"

"You know what I mean."

He's not here because he's worried about me or because he's unhappy about Morrison. He thinks

I killed Morrison but I'm in the hospital. Why does he think…?

"How did I get here?"

"When we came to get you this morning, you fainted again."

His voice is getting stronger, the anger even more apparent as he continues to speak to me. He's starting to scare me. I don't want to call a nurse, but I may need help.

"Where is my family?"

"They're in the waiting room with the doctor. No one is going to help you, Ria Sterling."

"What day is it?"

"It's Sunday morning."

And with those words, the missing day comes back to me. When I touched Morrison on Friday night, I collapsed on the hallway floor. Morrison went off to call an ambulance; Jones crouched down beside me.

"I'm okay. Don't call an ambulance. I'll phone my family."

Jones stared down into my eyes. He knew I was lying. Again. So I couldn't use my standard low blood sugar excuse. I waited. This time, Jones gave in.

"Morrison? She's okay. I'm going to call her family to come over and watch her."

"I'll call," I said. "Just give me a minute."

It wasn't easy but I pushed myself up onto my knees, then to my feet, holding onto the door handle for balance. I almost fell again when Morrison passed by, but he didn't touch me this time, and I managed to control my sorrow.

Jones watched me as I dialled home and reached Aunt Lucy.

"Aunt Lucy?"

I need to say nothing more. The trembling in my limbs has quickly been translated into my voice and my family knows the dangers of my gifts better than me. I'd lived with the pain, but they'd watched it almost kill me.

"Ria? I'll be right over. Joan and Gran are out for dinner. Shall I stop and get them?"

"No, it's not important. I just need one of you here. I'll tell you all about it when I see you."

I turn to Jones.

"That was my aunt. She's on her way over."

Jones nods.

"You don't need to wait."

I open the door and stand back. Jones shrugs his shoulders. The two of them sit in their car outside the house until Aunt Lucy drives up to take me home for the rest of the weekend.

I remember now.

Saturday had been a normal day. Lunch with a friend, one client I couldn't help, shopping with Mom for clothes for Gran. Pizza and red wine for dinner. And then I went home.

Fatcat waited on the front step. I'd forgotten him the night before and he was mightily pissed off. His tail lashed the dust from the stoop and his claws gouged three stripes in my leg.

"I'm so sorry," I said and held up a tin of tuna processed in oil. "I've brought you a treat."

The sound of the can opener stopped him from adding bite marks to the scratches. Fatcat had his priorities and food was at the top of the list. I left him purring on the kitchen counter and went upstairs to bed.

Saturday night I dreamed of trees crashing around me and birds falling from the sky. When a fist banged on my door in the middle of the night, I couldn't distinguish reality from the dream. By the time I got downstairs, Carrick Jones' boot had left dents in the oak door. I opened the door and he fell in.

"Ria Sterling? You're under arrest for the murder of Francis James Morrison. Anything you say…"

I tuned out the rest of his speech. Like everyone, I'd heard it hundreds of time on TV and in the movies. He wasn't telling me anything I didn't already know. I knew Frank Morrison was dead, and I knew Carrick Jones thought I did it. Obviously, so did at least one judge and the whole team of cops ranked behind Jones.

"My phone call?"

"At the station," he growled.

The station could have been transplanted directly from a TV set. Saturday night, full moon, and plenty of drunks and crazies. The noise grabbed me by the scruff of the neck and ripped whatever coherent thoughts I had from my head. Jones ushered me into a cell and locked me in.

"I'll be back in a few minutes," he said.

"My phone call?" I repeated.

"Soon."

That's the last thing I remembered before I woke up in a hospital bed.

"MS. STERLING? A NURSE pops her head in through the door and takes a quick look at Carrick Jones hulking over my bed. "Are you okay?"

I release the tension from my hands and check the panic button. I haven't pushed it, but it's still nestled in my palm. I want to know what's happened more than I want to feel safe.

"I'm fine. But can you tell my family I'm awake?

They'll be worried." The nurse smiles and waves as she backs out the door.

"Now tell me," I say. "What happened?"

"You tell me."

I take a close look at Carrick Jones while I'm waiting for him to decide whether to talk to me. He's a big man, filling out his t-shirt and jeans with muscle. His dark hair is starting to grey at the edges and he doesn't often get to the barber. The hair curls up over his collar. I remember his eyes from Friday, they are still the brilliant blue of the waters around Greece, but now they have iced over, like a glacier landed smack dab in the middle of the Mediterranean.

He is attractive in a rough kind of way, but right now he just looks mean.

This doesn't matter to me. My attraction to him exists at a much deeper level than his expression or his body. The minute he walked in the door of my house, I knew he was meant to be there, we were meant to meet. And it doesn't matter that he views my gift with disdain, even contempt, or that he seems to despise me.

It is hard to tell which of us is more stubborn but in the end I win this battle, mostly because I don't have anything to tell. All I know is that Morrison is dead. But I knew that on Friday night when I looked at his photograph. And confirmed it when he brushed by me.

"Detective Morrison was murdered, wasn't he?"

I keep my voice slow and quiet and my eyes down, remembering the skills Aunt Lucy taught us from her time working with abused dogs. *Don't challenge them,* she'd say, *they attack when you do.*

Carrick's head comes up and I hear the tears he's repressing when he speaks.

"It had to be someone he knew. He'd never have let a stranger get that close."

"Why do you think it's me?"

He doesn't have to say it; I know exactly what he's thinking. *Are you crazy? You told me he was going to die twenty-four hours before it happened. Of course you did it.*

I'm not sure why he chooses to speak to me now but I'm sure he has a plan. He's been a cop for a lot of years and it shows in his deliberate way of speaking, the weighing of each word I speak, each gesture I make. It shows when he looks at me, or at the nurse who comes in with a trolley of mid-morning drinks. It shows because, no matter how upset he is about Morrison's death, the grief almost doesn't show on his face.

I see it because I have experience. All the things

he's learned by being a cop, I've learned through using my gift. I've seen that haunted expression hundreds of times over the years.

He is pale and his eyes are red, with heavy bags under them. His hair stands up in clumps. But all those things might be lack of sleep. But his cheeks and jaw? That only ever happens with grief. It's as if someone has taken a knife and pared away three or four layers of tissue, leaving a face that no longer quite fits its owner. His skin is too tight on his face, stretched on a set of bones too big to accommodate it.

"I didn't kill him, you know. I don't even know how he died."

Jones holds out a plastic bag containing the envelope with his name written on it in my handwriting. He holds out another bag containing my note.

Detective Morrison is going to die. Within a day.

"You opened it before Monday?"

"Please, Ms. Sterling. I opened it in the car before we left. I showed it to Frank. He laughed. I did, too."

The thought of that laughter is too much for him and he turns away from me. If he'd taken my warning more seriously, maybe even believed in my gift, he might have saved Frank.

"You couldn't have saved him, you know. I've been trying for years and haven't been able to do it."

But I can see that he believes it's his fault. Because he didn't take me seriously, Morrison died. Carrick blames himself. Whether I killed Morrison or not, he blames himself, because either way he could have saved him.

I want to reach out to him but I remember his earlier reaction and restrain myself.

"You didn't believe in me. Or my gift."

I don't know why I'm still surprised, why, even with all the evidence, he still chooses not to believe. Carrick Jones is no different than any other cop. He doesn't believe in witches or the second sight. He doesn't believe in gypsies or anything else he can't touch. He would deny he has hunches, certainly deny that psychics might play a part in solving a crime. He thinks I'm a fraud and a liar. He even thinks I might be a murderer. And I don't blame him.

Because if things had turned out differently, if I had not got the help I needed when I needed it, I might have been anything. I think I had two choices. And if it weren't for Mama Amata I would either be dead or I would be in an asylum. I didn't want to believe in the gift. But Mama Amata convinced Aunt Lucy and Gran and they convinced Mom. I don't think it was too hard—they had all the evidence they needed right there in my bedroom.

But Carrick Jones refuses to believe the evidence he has about my gift, refuses to believe what the note is actually telling him. He's turning it around so it doesn't offend his logical left brain world. Evidence, actual physical evidence, is his god. If he can't see it, it can't be true. The note isn't enough.

"The only way you could know Frank was going to die was if you planned to kill him. All that mumbo-jumbo—your gift, your sight—means nothing. And the Chief backs me on this. Whatever he might have thought before, he knows you now. Just like I do. I know you killed Frank and I will make sure you end up exactly where you belong. In jail. Life without parole."

But it isn't that easy. I sense the guilt he carries for not having protected Frank. The guilt is pushing him deeper and deeper into an abyss he sees, but cannot resist. He's falling and can't stop himself. He's wavering underneath the bluster but he's trying desperately to ignore that other, weaker self.

And to confuse matters more, the longer we spend together, the stronger our mutual attraction. If I could put this attraction away for a short time, I would. It only makes matters worse. Carrick sees this attraction as a pull toward evil, toward the wicked woman who has murdered his partner. He feels himself turning toward the dark side and so he becomes even more adamant about my guilt.

I don't know how to get past the wall he's erected, but, if I am to avoid jail, if we are to have any kind of relationship, I need to do it. And I need to do it soon.

If he charges me with murder, it won't matter that I am not guilty. He'll forever believe I do not trust him. *How can she?* he'll think, *I'm the man who put her behind bars*. We have to get past that and we have to do it now.

"How did Frank die?" Again, I speak slowly and quietly, trying not to pull him out of his reverie.

He laughs.

"You have got to be shitting me. What do you think I am? A complete idiot? I am not telling you anything. I ask the questions, not you. You are the suspect, the prime and only suspect. As soon as the doctor says it's okay, you're coming back to the station with me to be questioned."

I give in.

"I need to call my lawyer. Now. Get out of my room."

He's shocked. I can't help myself, I laugh back at him.

"Do you think *I'm* an idiot? I'm not coming back

to the station without a lawyer. I'm not being questioned without a lawyer. Now get the hell out of my room. You'll hear from my attorney."

CHAPTER 5

Mom and Aunt Lucy don't want me to go into the house by myself, but I send them home. I need to call Uncle Jim and I need to get back to the station before the end of the day because if I don't, Carrick Jones will be on my doorstep. His patience is already exhausted and if I don't show up, he'll see it as me ignoring his authority. He'll be even more royally pissed off.

Fatcat isn't waiting at the door for me nor is he in the kitchen—his usual haunt.

"Fatcat? Come on, baby. I've got tuna for you."

I turn on the electric can opener, but Fatcat doesn't appear. Maybe Mom or Gran let him out this morning. But there is something else. A faint black sheen on almost everything in my white on white kitchen.

Damn. Damn. Damn. The cops have been here and Jones didn't tell me. I race through the rest of the rooms on the main floor, my fingers getting progressively blacker as I touch something in each room to be sure. The banister on the stairs wears its own veil of black, and so do the closet doors, the bathroom, even my bedroom. I'm going to kill that man. I'll strangle him. Or I'll use a knife. A knife would be good. No, the best thing would be a good kick in the balls. What the hell was he thinking?

I know exactly what he was thinking and my anger vanishes as quickly as it arrived. He thinks I killed Frank Morrison but thinking I'm a murderer doesn't make him want me any less. That makes two of us. I think he's an ass, but I still want him.

I open the back door and call again for Fatcat but there's no sign of him. It's odd, because since he showed up, he's never wandered far. It's as if he's decided that his territory covers the house, the front yard as far as the sidewalk, and the back yard right down to the old oak tree, but not a step further.

"Fatcat?"

I hear a weak meow from the basement door. I rip it open and Fatcat falls out of the door and onto my feet. I pick him up and, for the first time since I've known him, he allows me to hold him.

"Poor baby. Those big nasty police really scared you, didn't they? Well, they won't be doing it again.

No way. Not ever. I don't care what it takes, I'm going to deal with this and I'm going to do it today. I have to work tomorrow."

I put him down next to the tuna and he begins to purr as the tuna disappears.

"Uncle Jim? It's Ria."

Jim Farrar isn't really an uncle but he is a very old friend of Gran's. They went to grade school together. He used to be head of the state bar association. Since he retired, mostly he plays cards and takes Gran across the state line a couple of times a month to the casino, but he's still one of the best attorneys in the country.

"I need your help," I say.

"Your grandmother called me," Jim says. "I'll be at your house in half an hour. I've already called this Detective Jones and he's expecting us at two-thirty. That gives us an hour. Put the coffee on, please."

I hold nothing back talking to Uncle Jim. There is nothing to hide, he already knows about my gift and Gran has filled him in on what little there is to know about my relationship (if you can call it that) with Detective Morrison.

"Pretty arrogant, don't you think? That note was a really bad idea. It's the only thing they have on you."

"Carrick made me mad, he was so contemptuous

and snotty. I just wanted to show him I really did have the gift. I wanted him to know I wasn't a fraud."

Jim nods but says nothing. He's waiting. And I know what he's waiting for.

"You're right, I know you're right. Mama Amata would be ashamed of me."

"I don't think your Mama Amata could ever be ashamed of you. None of your family," he touches himself on the chest to say that includes him, "could ever, under any circumstances, be ashamed of you."

Uncle Jim rubs my shoulder and I lean into him. He's a little frail now but it isn't the size or strength of him that I love. He comforts me. He has been there for me whenever I needed him, my surrogate father. He took me to father-daughter events, gave me driving lessons, watched out for me when I started dating.

He is the only person I've ever told about my connection to my father, that I see him in the mirror when I look at myself, that he answers my questions. Jim understood how much I needed both him and my father as a child, and understands now how I feel about Carrick Jones.

Mom, Aunt Lucy and Gran allow me to do what I must, but they worry about me. And so they're uncomfortable about Carrick Jones. Uncle Jim is more confident about my abilities, less nervous about my mistakes. He believes I'll live through them and learn the lessons I need to learn.

The women in my family don't want me hurt, no matter what lesson I might learn from the pain. Carrick Jones looks to them like a pile of hurt.

"Thanks," I say.

"But what is it about this man that made you do such a thing?"

I don't know that I can tell him, don't know that I understand it myself. But I try. With Uncle Jim, I always try.

"There's something about him, something captivating. He's not handsome, at least not in any regular way, but he's attractive. I've never seen him when he wasn't mad at me, but he's got a kind of warmth that I've never seen in another man. And he's got these amazing eyes…"

"Thanks, missy, that's more than enough. You're attracted to him, you want to impress him, you want him to be attracted to you."

"Oh, it's not about that. He's already attracted to me, just like I am to him. There's no question about that. But I want him to be attracted to me because he wants to be, not because he can't help himself. Right now he hates me. I mean, he thinks I murdered his partner. And he still wants me. That's why he's mad. That's why he can't see reason."

Jim nods. I know he'll take this into account and be as careful as he can with Jones. Because in all the years he's known me, I've never been serious about a man. I've dated men, even slept with a few of them, but it was all pretty casual. I can see Jim storing up this information to tell Gran when he sees her next.

"You don't have to tell her," I say. "The three of them figured it out the minute they saw him. Sparks, they said, sparks everywhere."

The Sunday afternoon version of the police station is quite different from the wild and crazy Saturday night version. It's quiet, but there's a low-key buzz following Jim and I through the hallway. I can't hear the words, but I know what they're saying to each other.

"She's the one who killed Frank."

"She even bragged about it, wrote Jones a note the night before it happened."

"Bitch."

"She won't last long."

"I'd love to be there to watch Jones rip her apart."

"Frank's wife is a mess."

"And those kids. What are they going to do without him?"

"Yeah, well, she'll get hers."

The anger is palpable, even Jim feels it as we head for the interrogation room. He takes my arm and tucks me up against his side.

"It'll all be over soon. Don't fret. And don't answer any questions unless I tell you to."

He's told me this at least fifteen times in the past half an hour but I nod and remind myself: *Don't talk unless Jim says so. Don't get mad. Don't show any expression no matter what you're asked. Don't volunteer information.*

I can't tell any longer what Jim's told me and what's from movies or books or *Miami Vice*. Doesn't matter, though, it all comes down to the same thing.

We don't have to convince Carrick Jones I didn't do it, although that would be good, all we have to do is convince him that he doesn't have a case against me. And then we need to convince him that he needs to look for other suspects.

The interrogation room is cold and the chair feels damp against my leg. I can see myself in the big mirror across the room. I must remember that it's a window, not a mirror, and that someone is watching me through it even though I can't see him. Jim shakes his head at the two men across the table.

"Detective Jones and? I don't think we've been introduced."

"I'm head of homicide, George York. I'll sit in on this interview if you don't mind."

"No, no, of course not. But I always like to know who's sitting across the table from me. And my client."

I look over at Carrick Jones. He looks even worse than he did this morning when he left my hospital room. Then he looked unhappy and angry and tired. Now he looks as if he's spent the last five days in a storm, huddled under an inadequate tarp with wet clothes and blisters under his soaking socks. He looks like hell.

But I try and ignore that while I listen to Jim setting out the rules of the interview.

"Ms. Sterling is here because she chooses to be. She isn't charged with anything."

Jim waits for Jones to nod at this statement.

"She wants to help you if she can, but if that is impossible, she wants her name cleared and for your detectives—" a stern look at George York "—to leave her the hell alone."

Jim doesn't swear often but when he does it always works. Coming out of his mouth, the word *hell* sounds like street language coming out of the mouth of your favorite old maid aunt. Both men sit up and pay attention.

"She's our only suspect. Plus she told us she was going to kill him."

Carrick's hand shakes as he shoves my note across the table, still encased in its plastic wrapper.

"No. She didn't tell you she was going to kill him. She told you he was going to die. Those are two completely different statements."

Contempt crosses Carrick's face. York, on the other hand, seems content with Jim's assessment of the note. I wonder why.

His fingers tapping on the note, Jones begins again.

"She—" pointing at me "—told me more than twenty-four hours before he died that Frank Morrison was going to die. She fainted when he touched her. Why would she do that unless she knew she was going to kill him and she reacted to that? She has no alibi for the time of his death. She's a fraud. She's been arrested on numerous occasions for defrauding the public."

"Ah, but she hasn't ever been charged. Or convicted. Has she?"

"It doesn't matter. It shows a history of fraud, of dishonesty, of unlawful conduct. That's all we need to go on."

"Not exactly," Jim says calmly. "You don't have a case at all, do you? Or you'd have arrested her instead of waiting for her to come into the station voluntarily.

"Mr. York? I'm sorry I don't know your rank so you'll forgive me for my impoliteness, but why are you sitting in on this interview? If this is such a cut and dry case, why are you here?"

"One of my men has been killed. I choose, always, to be involved in those cases." York looks down at his hands and then across at Jim as if waiting for something.

"That's not the only reason, is it?"

I wonder where he's going and I can see that Carrick is wondering the same thing. His glance at George York is more confused than anything else.

"No, it's not the only reason, though what I've already told you is true. I know of Ria Sterling. I don't think she's capable of murder. But Detective Jones does believe that, and he has reasonable grounds for doing so. I want to make sure everything that can be explored is explored."

Now Carrick is very confused. I want to know how York knows about me. I don't wait for Jim's permission.

"How do you know me?"

"My baby sister was being stalked by her ex-boyfriend. He'd call every couple of days, drop around to her house at least once a week. *I'll kill you*, he'd say, *if I ever catch you with anyone else. I'll kill him, too*. She didn't tell me about it, didn't want me to do anything stupid. But when he vanished, she called me.

"She was a mess. She accused me of killing him. *I'll confess*, she said, *it's my fault. I know you did it for me.* I told her I didn't do it, didn't even know what she was talking about. But she was spooked, didn't believe me for a long time.

"But we couldn't find him. Couldn't find where he'd gone, what he was doing. It was as if he'd disappeared from the face of the earth. I don't know, aliens maybe. That's how complete his disappearance was. Now I'm a cop, and I have a lot of resources, but I couldn't find a sign of him.

"All the while my baby sister is losing weight. She can't eat. She can't sleep. She can't go to work. Every time I see her, there is less of her. Less physically and less emotionally. She's dying and I can't do a thing about it.

"So I send her to you. A guy at the gym knew your name, knew where you lived, and he said you were the real thing.

"And you tell her that the bum is going to die. And she believes you. She can eat again, sleep, go back to work. It took almost a year for word to filter back that he'd died in an accident somewhere in Mexico. And he'd died the very day she saw you.

Maybe it's a coincidence. But I'm willing to take a chance on it. I've checked you out since then, Ms. Sterling. Sounds like the real thing to me."

Carrick Jones shakes his head in disbelief. "What the hell are you thinking, George?"

George smiles at him. "I'm keeping an open mind. You might try it, too. I'm outta here. Ms. Sterling. Mr. Farrar."

The door closes behind him with a finality that I find frightening but Uncle Jim seems to find satisfying.

"Now we can get to it," he says. He's not actually doing it but I sense he would be rubbing his hands in glee if he didn't think it rude.

"How did Detective Morrison die?"

I shake my head. As if Carrick Jones is going to tell us that. That's all he's got to catch me up. And I'm right. He doesn't answer.

"When did he die?"

That's an easier question for him to answer. I don't have an alibi at all for Saturday night.

"Just after nine on Saturday night."

"Good. Good. Now we're getting somewhere." Jim's hands clasp until he realizes what he's doing.

"Where did he die?"

It can't be too far. I couldn't go to another state or even across this one to kill him. I didn't have enough time to go more than a couple of hundred miles between Mom and Aunt Lucy leaving and Carrick arriving on my doorstep to take me to jail. He'll answer this one as well.

"He died in his car. Parking lot behind Joe's Diner on Fifth."

"Hmmmm."

I don't have any idea where Uncle Jim is going with all this but at least Carrick's speaking. That has to be a good thing.

"Okay. I have here," Uncle Jim pulls a sheaf of paper from his briefcase, "letters of endorsement from citizens from all over this country. People who have been helped by Ria Sterling. People who know that she knew things she couldn't have known without the gift. One of them—" he waves a letter at Carrick "—is from the governor's brother. This one—" he pulls another out of the pile "—is from a world famous actor. And this one is from your mother."

I don't know who is more surprised, me or Carrick. When did Uncle Jim collect all these letters?

"My mother?"

"Your mother. She wanted to know about her best friend from high school. When she didn't show up at their twenty-fifth reunion, your mother got worried. She came to Ria. Ria told her that her friend was going to die and the very next day she got a call from the friend's husband that the woman had died of cancer the night before."

While Carrick is thinking that over, I whisper at Uncle Jim.

"Why? And when? I can't believe you did this."

"Your Gran and I decided about ten years ago that you might one day get into some more serious trouble with the law than the usual fraud charges. So we started collecting the letters. She's smart, your Gran, huh?"

"She is."

But now I am seriously worried about Carrick Jones. His breathing has become rapid and shallow. There is not a single patch of color left in his face.

This time I don't stop myself. I reach across the table and put my hand on his. It is very cold and that scares me. I pull his hand into mine and wrap the other around it, rubbing it to warm him.

"Carrick?" I whisper. "Carrick?"

He raises his head and I am shocked by the intensity of the blue of his eyes. Brighter than any sky, brighter than any blue I've ever seen. And in his pale face, they shine like strobe lights in the desert night.

"Carrick?"

"You've met my mother? Why didn't she tell me?"

"I don't know why she didn't tell you. Does it matter?"

Jim shushes me. "That's enough, Ria."

I stop talking but I continue holding onto Carrick's hand. It is getting warmer in my hands and I concentrate on that, willing the warmth to shoot up his arm and into his heart. Willing him to change his mind about me.

"How did Frank Morrison die?" Jim asks again.

"You know I can't tell you that."

"Yes, I know, but I want you to think about how he died. Now look at my client. Could she have done it?"

And now it is obvious that Uncle Jim has been manoeuvring the entire conversation around to this one question. He has done everything needed to get Carrick to this point, to a willingness to consider *this* question. Somehow Uncle Jim has discovered how Detective Morrison was killed.

"Show him your hands, Ria. Detective Jones, look at her hands. Could she have killed Detective Morrison?"

Carrick puts his hand on top of mine, then turns them both over. He studies them as carefully as if they were Venetian glass. He touches the mounds at the base of my thumbs, makes a fist around my baby finger, then my ring finger, then my middle finger.

He takes my right hand and encloses it within his left, then does the same with my left hand. He has been looking down at our linked hands but now he raises his face to mine.

Suddenly, he looks as if he has had eight hours sleep, two cups of coffee and the best breakfast in town. When he smiles at me, my heart responds by trying to beat its way out of my chest.

"No, she couldn't have done it. Of course she couldn't have done it."

"Will someone please tell me what just went on in here?" My patience has expired. I know we've won but I don't understand the game.

"What are you two grinning about?"

Uncle Jim is the one who answers.

"Frank Morrison was killed with a very large and very heavy machete. You could pick it up, you're very strong, but you certainly couldn't wield it the way it was used to kill Detective Morrison without leaving serious blisters on your hands. Your hands aren't large enough to have killed him.

"Detective Jones?"

"But I'm a welder," I say. "I wield large equipment every single day. I can bench press almost two hundred pounds. I'm strong."

And I'm offended that female weakness is what

gets me off the murder charge. I want to be set free because I'm innocent, not because I'm too small to commit the damned murder. My disgust must show in my face because both Uncle Jim and Carrick Jones laugh, but only Jim answers me.

"A welding torch or wand is one thing, and besides, I know you have your tools specially made for your small hands. The machete," he looks across at Carrick for permission to continue, who nods, "wasn't just your regular everyday machete. The blade was grafted onto a handle that was at least eight inches across. You couldn't have wielded it."

Both men look pointedly at my small hands.

"Your uncle's right. I'll get you out of here. We won't be bothering you again."

Carrick rips his hands from mine and stands up. The air in the room turns cold again. I see where this is going.

"Uncle Jim? Can you leave us alone for a minute? And can you make sure there's no one left in that room as well?"

I wave at the mirrored wall.

"Turn off the tape machines, too, okay?"

Uncle Jim smiles and salutes.

"I'll wait outside for you. Don't be too long, I

have a dinner date with your Gran and you know what she's like when I'm late."

I wait a few minutes to make sure we're alone.

"Carrick Jones, it's time you and I had a little chat."

CHAPTER 6

"Not now. I have to…"

"No, you don't. Someone else is already looking for Frank's killer."

"Not like I would be if I weren't so distracted."

"You're distracted because Frank was your partner. And don't they take you off the case if it was your partner killed?"

"That's only in movies. I know what Frank was doing better than anyone else. I'm the one who'll find his killer."

I sigh. This man is as stubborn as I am and that's some stubborn. But I'm not giving up. Not yet.

"Five minutes, okay? That's all."

The moments it takes for him to make up his mind seem to last forever. Jones is the kind of cop whose emotions never show on his face, and I don't know how it is that I can read him, but I can. Every emotion passing over his face is clear to me, as clear as if I were feeling them myself. *Guilt*. I think that's at the top of his emotional landscape. Then *confusion*.

He keeps asking himself, *What does Ria Sterling want?* A little bit of hope, quickly dispelled by anger. It's my fault he hasn't been looking for Frank's killer. And finally, underneath it all and totally implacable, *desire*. He wants me. In the end, lucky for me, the hope and the desire win out. Temporarily.

"Five minutes." He looks at his watch and settles in his chair, leaning back far enough that he's balancing on the two back legs. He crosses his arms. "Go."

Gulp. It's up to me.

"I think I can help you find Frank's killer."

"Oh?"

"Yes. Frank was the very first…" I pause because I don't know what to call him. Victim? Client? Dead person? "Frank is the only person I've actually touched once I knew they were going to die. I had an extreme reaction."

"Yes?"

His stand-offish attitude is starting to piss me off. I get up and walk over to his side of the table. I childishly push on the back of his chair but he's too fast for me. He grabs my wrists, pulls me in front of him and leans forward. His arms are on both sides of me, trapping me against the cold metal table.

"Carrick?"

I lean forward and lean my head against his. Our hearts are beating exactly in tandem, I can feel mine and his, too. It's weird but also oddly satisfying.

"Carrick?"

His arms come off the table and around my waist. He holds me as if I'm all that is standing between him and hell, and maybe I am. I pull him closer and wait for him to say something.

"You can't help me, you know. This isn't about some magic or some *gift*."

He spits out the word as if it sickens him. It does. I know it does. It sickens everyone around me, even me sometimes. It's a useless gift and I hate having it. But I can't get rid of it. God knows I've tried. Therapy. Hypnosis. Yoga. Drugs. Alcohol. None of them work. And now Carrick Jones despises me because of my gift. That's the emotion that I have to fight.

He desires me, but it's against his will. And he won't do anything about it. He pulls away and stands up, his head averted. The smell of him stays in my nostrils. It will never go away.

"Ria. Go on home. I've got work to do."

Whatever I thought I might say to him, whatever I thought might break through the barrier between us, is gone. And so am I.

I go home and start my Sunday night ritual. Working as a welder is what keeps me sane. I have to focus every minute of the day and that's good for me. I can't be worrying about the people I can't help.

I can't be brooding about Carrick Jones.

So I check my equipment, pack my bag, make my lunch, sit zazen for an hour. It doesn't dispel the past few days, but it does help me deal with it. I still feel Frank's death, still feel Carrick's heart beating, but I can put them aside for now.

In the morning, the radio news—I don't get a paper, of course—says the department is looking into Frank's murder but they have no comment—read that, as Carrick Jones would put it, no fucking clue— at this time.

"Detective York has denied that this is the case and has said that the department has a task force working on the matter and expects to have further information shortly."

I laugh at the irony of the report, but there's nothing I can do about it. I pick up my bag and hurry out to my truck. The job site is on the other side of town and I don't want to be late. This is a tough job and being late will make everything worse.

We're building a new medical center for people who live on the east side of town. Up until now, they've had to traipse right through downtown and over here to the west side to see a doctor or a dentist or a therapist. But we've grown enough in the past ten years that Marathon thinks it can make a go of another center. I hope they're right, but even if they're not, I've got a steady six months' worth of work.

Working construction means I often don't know where my next job is coming from. Being a female welder means I've had to bite my tongue on hundreds of occasions in order to keep working. Construction is a rough job for a woman, and welding even tougher. But I hide behind my mask, wear big heavy clothes, and I get by.

I love the work. Love the way the torch feels in my hand, love the perfect joins I make with it, love the sparks and the faint hint of danger I feel every minute I'm working. I love all the different types of welding: torch brazing, arc welding, soldering. They're all different but they all have one thing in common. When I'm finished, if I've done it right, I have a perfect join and I can see and feel that perfection.

I haven't worked for Marathon before this job but they're a big company. Getting on with them might make my life a whole lot easier over the next few years. They're throwing up buildings all over the city. If they like me, I might never be out of work again.

Ria Sterling, eternal optimist.

My first day with Marathon and every one since then has been hell. If it weren't for the fact that I don't have another job to go to, my mortgage payment is due, and I need a new roof, I would have quit every single day.

The job site is unsafe. Scary unsafe, not just a few ignored regulations, but deep problems. I am working with three kids, and I mean kids. I ask one of them what welding experience he has and he says, "Oh, I've done a bit around the house." I think the other two are even worse. Now I not only have to watch myself, I have to watch them as well.

We didn't accomplish much that first day, but neither did anybody else. For a fast track project, this building is going up at a snail's pace.

Fatcat is cowering under the bed again when I get home from work. Those damned cops. If they've permanently traumatized Fatcat… What am I going to do? Nothing to do.

After my shower, I throw my stinking damp clothes into the washing machine and sit down at the computer. The half hour under the hot water didn't do anything to take the kinks out of my neck today. Thank God I don't have any messages, nothing to worry about.

I pull up my accounting program and try to figure out a way to make it through the next few weeks if I quit Marathon. There isn't one. The roof has to be done before the winter rains, and I have only enough put away for one mortgage payment. So I have to stay with Marathon, and live through a few weeks of hell until I find another job.

The next day isn't any better; in fact, it's worse. The foreman is a real asshole and he has no patience with the three guys I'm working with. He hired them and should know they're green, but he doesn't care. First, he fires Jason, leaving two inexperienced men and one woman to do the work of five. Later on in the day, he comes up behind Fred and scares him into dropping his torch. Fred's gone too.

Now there are only two of us, me and Kenny. Kenny's the one who says he's welded at home sometimes. I'd be willing to bet that those sometimes were maybe once, and that was while his daddy was holding his hand. But I need him. This is a rush job and I can't do it all myself. As it is, I'm working my ass off, and not making much progress.

I'm going to have to talk to the foreman.

"Mr. Dunning?"

I know he knows who I am—the only female welder within a fifty mile radius—but I introduce myself anyway.

"I'm Ria Sterling. I'm your head welder on this job."

"Yeah, waddaya want?"

He turns away from me, his beefed up shoulders and back blocking my view of his face. He's at least a foot taller than me and I can't see anything except his shoulders.

"Mr. Dunning, we need some more welders. We can't keep up, just the two of us."

"You can't keep up? Well, what are you doing standing here talking to me? Get that pretty ass of yours back on the job and quit whining to me."

It isn't easy, but I turn my back without screaming at him. The words are locked in my throat and I can't speak at all when I get back to Kenny. He throws a questioning look my way and I shrug. He gets back to work. And so do I.

Eventually Kenny and I get into a rhythm of a kind. We're still miles behind where we should be but we're doing the best we can. Moving fast, but I won't let Dunning or Kenny make us take shortcuts. I do all the complicated welds, the ones up in the corners, the ones hidden halfway behind another piece of pipe. I also do all the crucial ones. I know

Kenny doesn't know what he's doing but I think he's okay to do the easy stuff. He has to be.

When I get out of bed on Wednesday morning, I know today is going to be even worse, because I'm stiff and aching. I must have a cold or the flu coming on and adding that to two twelve-hour days of working all out means I can hardly move this morning. Lucky I got out of bed early, at least I can have a hot bath before I try to do too much.

The hot bath saves me. I can move, albeit gingerly, and my aches have disappeared behind a veil of ibuprofen and tiger balm. I still have a headache, but it's not serious.

The gift has meant that I live with headaches. Not every day, and not often when I don't have to use it, but three or four times a week I wake up with one. Sometimes it means a person is going to show up to ask questions, sometimes it just means a headache. I hope today is just a headache. I don't think I can deal with a grieving mother on top of everything else.

And I haven't heard from Carrick Jones. Not a single word. The radio just keeps saying the same thing, they're working on it, and Uncle Jim has vanished with Gran for another casino trip so I can't ask him.

Before I can change my mind, I pick up the phone and dial his number.

"Detective Jones."

"Carrick, it's Ria."

"Yes?" His voice is tentative, as if he doesn't quite remember who I am.

"Ria, Ria Sterling."

"Yes, I know who you are. What do you want?"

"God, Carrick Jones, you are a real asshole, you know?"

I slam down the phone and run out the door. I hear it ringing behind me but I don't go back. He is an asshole and I can't be bothered to talk to him this morning.

It's hot and humid and I feel a storm coming. Maybe that's where my headache comes from. The bad news is that this'll make things go from bad to worse at work. Long sleeves, heavy gloves, a full face mask. It'll be a hundred and ten degrees in working clothes. Shit.

And when I get to work, Kenny's missing.

"Mr. Dunning, where's Kenny?"

"He called in sick this morning. You'll have to work on your own today. So get to it, lady. Now."

He points over at the slowly growing building and I follow his finger. No point in yelling at him. It won't get me anywhere except fired. Or maybe not, I think. I'm the only one left and he can't do without me. But he's not smart enough to remember that when his temper flares.

Just like Carrick Jones. Men. Sometimes I think I'd like to... What? Give them up? Not Carrick Jones even though I still have no idea how to get around his barriers.

Today I'm working on the third floor in the back corner. I'm the only one up here and I'm grateful for that small favor. The men on this site haven't been easy on me. They're always coming up behind me and touching my shoulder or my arm. I know they realize they can't touch my butt without getting fired, Dunning made that clear at the beginning, but they have no hesitation about scaring the hell out of me three or four times a day.

I've tried telling them what a bad idea that is when I'm holding a welding torch, but they don't listen. They just keep coming up and scaring me, waiting for me to drop the torch or screw up a weld and get fired.

Carrick Jones. What is it with that man, anyway? Why can't he just acknowledge what is sparking between us? It's so obvious to me. Maybe if we just jump into bed together it'll go away, he'll go away, and I'll be fine. Maybe I'll try calling him again tonight and suggesting that. Why not? He's ruining my life anyway. What's the worst that can happen? He says no. He's saying that already.

The thoughts won't leave me today. Usually, just picking up the torch calms me and I focus without any effort. But today, Dunning and Carrick Jones and the jerks on this job site keep interfering with my focus, slowing down my work.

"Shit, you ass. You almost got blinded right there," I scream at the dark figure I glimpse over my shoulder.

And then it's too late. He's grabbed my mask, and the gas arcs through the air in front of my eyes. I hear his footsteps racing away and I scream for what seems like hours, until someone comes and finds me lying on the ground. My hands are over my eyes.

"I can't see," I scream. "I can't see."

CHAPTER 7

Same hospital, different room. At least it sounds different. I still can't see anything. Think about something else. Okay, how's this? I've been in the hospital more since I met Carrick Jones than in my entire life, except for that time when I was fifteen.

Someone has pinned the button to my hand and I press it. Once. No one shows up. Twice. Still no one. Again.

And I scream.

"Where is everyone? Please? Someone? I can't see."

I can't even tell if I'm crying, I just know that my eyes hurt.

"Help me. Someone."

I'm pressing the button like crazy but no one is coming. What time is it? Where am I? I know why I can't see, that damned dark man at the job site scared me. And then he pulled off my mask. Just another welding accident, right? And there goes my job...

"Someone, please. Please."

I feel more than hear the door open. The air in the room changes and I stop screaming, staying still, not even breathing.

"Who's there?"

"Ria?"

I'd expected my family but it is Carrick Jones who sits down on the chair next to my bed. Now that he's this close I can smell him and I take a deep breath, taking his aroma into my lungs. It calms me, a bit.

"Where's the doctor? Where I am? What does my chart say?"

I wave down to where I think the foot of the bed is and say, "Pick that up, will you, and tell me what it says? Carrick? Come on? I need to know."

"You're going to be okay."

"I am?"

"Yes. Maybe ten days, he says. It usually takes that long for the eyes to mend, but he's going to check in a week or so. They're burned, but not too badly.

"How did it happen?" he asks, voice casual.

"I need to see the doctor. I want to know what's going on. I can't be blind. I need to get back to work. Get him. Get him now."

A hand touches my hair so lightly I'm not sure if

I am imagining it. "I'll go get him now. Your Mom and Aunt Lucy are outside. I'll send them in."

When he arrives, the doctor reassures me, but tells me I won't be able to take off the bandages for at least a week. I can go home tomorrow, but I'll need someone with me, he says, because I'll be blind. Yeah, sure, I guess I didn't notice that.

Both Mom and Aunt Lucy volunteer to stay with me, but I hesitate. Maybe I need to be by myself, wallowing in my own misery without someone trying to cheer me up all the time.

"Ria, don't be stubborn. You can't stay in that house all by yourself when you can't see." I hear the worry in Mom's voice.

"The doctor says you have to have someone," Aunt Lucy chimes in.

"Let me talk to Detective Jones," I say. "Maybe he can stay with me."

"We'll be right outside the door." Aunt Lucy rushes Mom out of the room.

Carrick Jones sits back down beside the bed and I take another deep breath. He smells great.

"Tell me what happened," he says.

This time, when I reach for his hand, he lets me take it. He wraps his warm fingers around my cold ones.

"What happened?"

"I don't know. I mean, I'm not sure. I'm careful, I'm always careful. I've been doing this for almost fifteen years and I've never had an accident."

"So this wasn't an accident."

I think again about the dark man.

"No, I don't think so."

"Tell me," his fingers tightening around my hand. "Tell me what happened. Start right at the beginning."

"I'm working on the new medical center across town. Marathon's a big company and I thought it would be a good job for me, six months of steady work. But it's been hell. Understaffed, a crew of jerks, pretty much as bad as it could be. I would have quit if it weren't for my new roof."

Damn. Now what am I going to do? Workers' comp isn't going to pay for a new roof.

"How long am I going to be off work?"

"I don't know, the doctor didn't say, at least to me he didn't say. Do you want me to go and ask him?"

"Not now." I tighten my hold on his fingers. "Don't go yet, okay?"

"Okay," he says. "I won't go until you say so."

"So Dunning fires two of the kids working with me, and on Wednesday, Kenny calls in sick. I have a head-ache, maybe a cold or the flu coming on." I take a breath and realize that, except for my eyes, I feel fine.

I know I should be more worried, but I know plenty of welders who've been flashed, and they're all fine.

"So I'm it, I'm tired, I'm angry, I'm thinking about you. It's going to be my third twelve- or fourteen-hour day and it's late in the afternoon. I'm up on the third floor by myself, everyone else is clocking out but I'm planning on another three or four hours, at least until the sun goes down.

"I hear somebody come up behind me and I know I tense up, 'cause I'm expecting somebody to slap me on the shoulder. I try to turn off the gas. I can remember reaching behind me to do it.

"And then someone rips off my mask. A flash, and I'm blinded. Takes forever for someone to hear me screaming, and forever for the ambulance to get there."

I shake as I tell this part of the story because it's every welder's greatest fear, that flash, and once you've seen it, it's too late. You're blind and you can't know how bad it'll be. Maybe a week or two, maybe a couple of months. Sometimes, rarely, it's forever.

"He didn't stay to help you?" Carrick asks.

And I wonder the same thing myself. Pranks are one thing, leaving a blind person on the top floor of an unfinished building is tantamount to murder. I start shaking the minute I think of the things that might have happened.

If I moved, even an inch, I'd have been over the edge. Down three stories into a muddle of steel and equipment. Tripped over a tool or a bucket or a wire. Fallen backwards into the torch, burning more than my eyes. Nightmare city. I'll be having them for months.

The screams come back up my throat but I suppress them. Who would do this? I don't realize it, but I start talking out loud.

"One of the fired welders?"

"I already checked," Carrick says. "Keep going."

"It has to be someone on site. But why? They tease me, play pranks on me, but I've been around construction workers for years. They're not mean."

"But who else?" He prods me.

"Maybe someone," I don't want to say it.

"Someone, who?" He's relentless.

"Someone who came to me—like your mom, I mean."

"Why?"

Carrick's cop persona is aggravating me.

"I don't know why," I spit. "It's all I can think of."

"Okay, what did he look like?"

"I don't know, the sun was behind him and all I saw was a dark silhouette. He was tall, I think, but that's about all I remember."

I'm content to sit there holding his hand but I remember Aunt Lucy and Mom out in the hallway.

"Carrick?"

"Hmmm?"

"Will you come and stay with me until I can see again?"

He rips his hand out of mine. I can hear him pacing, and I know he doesn't know what to say. He doesn't want to hurt my feelings but he thinks this is really a bad idea. Mr. Stand-off, that's who he is.

"Carrick? I'm scared."

Okay, so I cheat a little. I'm not really scared. Maybe, I hope, the guy was just one of the crew, out to frighten me a little more than usual. And he left because he was scared of the consequences. But I'll use anything to get Carrick into my house.

"You don't need to be afraid. Your family can stay with you. Or you can stay with them."

"Nope. I can't move Fatcat. He's so traumatized from your search the other day, he hardly comes out from under the bed. Forget it. I'll get one of them to stay with me. No problem. Really."

I have my fingers crossed when I say this. This is my big chance with Carrick Jones and I'm not going to waste two weeks with the family when I can take advantage of my disability.

"Thanks for dropping by."

"I'm going to go down to the construction site and see if I can figure out who did this to you. There's not much I can do about it, but I'll make sure it doesn't happen again."

He doesn't touch me this time when he leaves, though he does stop by the bed for a moment. I can smell him, even hear him breathing, and if I really concentrate, I'm sure I can feel his heart beating.

"Mom? Aunt Lucy? I need a favor."

When I get home, Fatcat comes to greet me. He only does that when I'm alone, but today he doesn't even slash at my ankles.

"Be careful, you. I can't see you so don't be getting under my feet." I swirl the cane around and come into contact with the stairs. "Okay, that's good. Now I know where I am."

It isn't easy to get up the stairs and into my bedroom, but I've spent plenty of nights wandering this house in the dark, so it's less difficult than anyone might expect. When I can't sleep, I can't read or watch TV either. And I definitely can't turn on the lights, so I tend to spend my many sleepless nights wandering around the house in the dark. And it is dark. No night lights, no street lights shining in the windows.

I like it that way. I don't want to be able to see myself in the windows or the mirrors. I don't want to see anything. What I want to do is wear myself out enough to go back to bed and sleep. It doesn't often work, but I keep trying.

Tonight, though, I have something else in mind. When the grandfather clock down the stairs chimes three, I pick up my phone and carefully dial a number.

"Yeah?"

"Carrick? It's Ria. I just heard something in my hallway."

"Where's your mother?"

"She couldn't come tonight. I'm here by myself."

Okay, okay, I'm lying about my mother, but it's justified. It's a little white lie—I did hear Fatcat prowling a few minutes ago.

"I'll be right over."

This time we *will* finish our conversation. No interruptions, no distractions, no walking away from me.

When his car pulls up, I open the door. Bad idea.

"What the hell do you think you're doing? I could have been anybody. A murderer. A rapist. A thief. And you open the door?"

"I know the sound of your car."

"Yeah, sure.

"I'm going to check the house out. Just sit here—"

he leads me to the living room "—and don't move. If you do, I might shoot you by mistake."

He sounds like he'd be happy to make that mistake. I guess I can't blame him. I've been a pain in the butt ever since he showed up on my doorstep.

Something compels me to force the connection between us. We need to work together. This is all I know, but I know it with every sense I have. What happens between us on a personal level may not matter except to my heart, but working together is crucial.

I wish Mama Amata was reachable. She might know what this means. It feels like my gift has taken over in a way it's never done before. The trouble is I can't read anything more than the emotional necessity of things; I knew that someone was going to arrive on my doorstep and that I had to be ready for it.

I hear Jones hit the squeaky floorboard in the attic, then the one outside my bedroom. The steps groan as he comes back down to the main floor, then the basement door screeches, first on his way down, then on his way back up into the kitchen.

"Hey, you," he's talking to Fatcat. "What are you doing hiding there?"

Fatcat will be under the table in the kitchen, his favorite place. Close to the food, but out of the way of intruders. I don't hear any screams or curses.

Fatcat hates everyone, including me, except, obviously, Jones. They're both tough guys, at least on the surface.

I smell him this time before I hear him. There are no telltale squeaks between the kitchen and here and he is light-footed for a man his size. I think for a minute about the way he moves, as if he were swimming through the air, his body almost weightless in its embrace. I shake my head.

"Jones? We need to talk."

He growls, sounding exactly like Fatcat when he's hungry or wanting to go out.

"We already did talk."

"No, we didn't, not really. Jones, you have to listen to me. I know you don't believe in my gift and I don't blame you. I've been living with it for almost thirty years and sometimes it still freaks me out. But you need to believe in me. What would it take?"

"Why do I need to believe in you?"

I can't explain it to him. It's kind of like childbirth or love—you need to feel it before you can believe it. No one can tell you what it's like, no one can explain how it feels, no matter how many words get used. But I have to keep trying.

"We need to work together…" He doesn't let me finish my sentence, hardly lets me begin it.

"Work together? What, you want to be my new partner now that Morrison's dead?"

"You know that's not what I mean."

"So what do you mean? Spit it out. And while you're at it, tell me what you're doing at home by yourself. You told me you'd get someone to stay with you. The cat doesn't count."

"I'm home by myself because I needed to talk to you without interruptions and this was the only thing I could think of."

"Bad idea. I'm surprised you haven't fallen down the stairs yet."

He's pacing around the room, six steps across, six steps back. The sound of his heels hitting the floor— right, left, right, left—punctuates my thoughts.

"I felt something on Friday night, before you got here. I knew I had to get prepared."

"For what?"

"Let me finish this, okay? Just let me get through it once and then you can pick all the holes you want."

He doesn't answer but at least he doesn't interrupt.

"There's a reason you showed up at my house on Friday night."

I can feel him wanting to say, *yeah, the chief sent me,* but he restrains himself and lets me go on.

"My gift hasn't ever allowed me but one thing. I see

death in photographs. I don't see it anywhere else, and I don't see it more than a few hours out from when I touch the photograph. I can't tell you if someone is already dead, only if they are going to die. Soon.

"But on Friday night I felt something different. Foreboding. Something bad is going to happen and the only way it can be stopped is if we work together."

This time he can't help himself.

"Something bad has already happened. You don't get any worse than dead."

"Morrison's part of it," I reply. "I think that's why I had such an intense reaction to his presence. But he's not all of it. More deaths, more pain. It's coming. I can't get any closer than that."

"You know, Ria, if I wasn't damn sure you didn't kill Morrison, I'd be taking you back down to the station. You're setting yourself up for a fall."

I know I'm taking a risk but I don't know how else to get through to him. Uncle Jim would be appalled if he knew what I was doing but he's safely at the casino with Gran. Mom and Aunt Lucy agree with me—they know I have to work this out.

"It's not about me, or you. I don't care if you throw me back in jail. I still have to try to save these people. I've been trying to do that all my grown up life. There's something about this situation—" I pause and then try again. "I feel like I'm close to expanding the whole thing. I can't give it up."

"Give what up? What do you think you can do? We can do together? You have absolutely nothing to go on except this vague feeling of yours."

"But that's more than I've ever had before.

"I always knew, right from the beginning, that there was nothing I could do to save them, to save anyone. I couldn't help because I never had enough information, never knew early enough. I could see them dying, but I couldn't see how or where or why. All I could see was death coming for them. I've spent my life knowing I was too late. Now I've been given a chance to change that. Maybe I can save someone."

I've been trying to get his attention, to get him to listen, really listen to me, and now Carrick's breathing has quickened to match mine.

"That's what I want," he says quietly. "A chance to save someone. Working homicide, it's all about death. Maybe you can save some perp's next victim, but you never really know. I've been thinking about going back on the street. When you're there, you see people living their lives, trying to get along. You can maybe stop them from getting burgled, find their lost daughter or car or stereo. In homicide, it's always too late."

I don't know if he can feel it, but it's as if the same

blood is flowing through both our veins. I can feel his heart beating with mine, and our breathing slows. I can't see him, but I'm closer to Carrick Jones than I've ever been. I know exactly where he is, what he looks like, even what he's thinking and feeling. For this short moment, we are one.

CHAPTER 8

And it is short. The moment, I mean. It can't be longer than sixty seconds before I hear him start to breathe again, and not in unison with me, either.

"Ria. Here," he places the phone in my hand. "Call your mother. I'll wait outside in the car until she gets here."

I know stubborn, and nothing is going to change Carrick Jones' mind. So I dial the house.

Mom and Aunt Lucy are up, waiting for me to call. They knew this wouldn't work, knew Jones better than me, and realized that his aversion to my gift is deeper than his attraction to me.

But I don't want it to be about only that. I want, God, how I want, to save someone, and I think the two of us can do it together. And when he confessed his desire to help people, that is my confirmation that it's right. That whatever it is that has changed my gift and given me insight, is right about the two of us working together and saving someone. We aren't going to save Lisa Alison Martin. I am pretty certain about that—she's been gone too long and Carrick's focused on Frank, not her.

And I know that how?

The trouble is that I can't convince Jones because I can't explain it, not even to myself.

Mom and Aunt Lucy are talking quietly in the kitchen. I feel the sun's warmth on my shoulders as I sit on the window ledge. I hear their voices and the sweet tinkle of their spoons against their cups, but I can't hear the words. They're happy to be here with me. They were already packed when I phoned.

I love it that they worry about me—they're my safety net for those times when I can't bear the gift alone—but today I need them to stay out of the way. I told them what I intended to do. They wanted to stay with me, but I told them no. What I'm going to try is best done alone.

I can't read the notes I scribbled after Mama Amata left me all those years ago, but I don't need to. I've memorized them. They're written on cheap yellow-lined pages, wrinkled, worn and spotted with tears and soda and food. They didn't start out that way. When I first wrote them down, they were pristine and perfect.

Whenever I get discouraged, whenever too many people show up and all I can see is death, I read my notes about her and what she told me. And I don't give up. Not for that one day.

Mostly she told me about seeing death, how it worked for her, how she dealt with it, but there's a piece at the end of the notes that I've never figured out.

"Ria," she said, filling in the first page of the yellow pad—the only one in her handwriting, "I am writing this down but I hope you will never need it. It is complicated and it is dangerous.

"I myself have never used it. My gift, like yours, is not a large one, but this information has come to me through the family. It has been passed down from grandmother to granddaughter for generations. I do not know whether any of those who went before us used it. The stories do not say."

Sitting with the sun on my shoulders, I remember the day Mama Amata left. I remember it as if it were yesterday, even though it's twenty years in the past. I see her sitting on the edge of my bed, her feet swinging inches above the carpet and her tiny hands wrapped around a steaming cup of herbal tea. She smelled like lemon and wild roses, still my favourite of all aromas.

"Ria, my darling," she said, "I have to leave now."

"You can't leave," I said, tears beginning to fall, "I need you." I touched my finger to my cheek and grabbed a glistening drop. "See? I'm crying again."

"Yes, but this time you are crying because I am leaving, not because of your gift."

I didn't know how she could tell the difference. It felt the same to me except that I wasn't hiccupping. She smiled at me.

"I can tell the difference because you are going to stop crying once I explain to you why it is that I must leave.

"Many people depend on me, Ria, just as they will come to depend on you. They know where to find me and they know that I will help them. I do not like to leave my home for long.

"You, my angel, are going to be perfectly fine. I promise."

And she was right. That is, if you think of perfectly fine as me sitting blind in my living room trying to get up enough nerve to follow her instructions and conjure up the spirit of Mama Amata.

Mama Amata died almost fifteen years ago. Her silhouette told me that the day it happened. It doesn't matter that I hadn't heard or seen from her since she walked out of my bedroom that day when I was fifteen, or that no one officially informed me of her death.

The black cardboard silhouette of her profile flared white when I touched it that morning. I stroked it for a moment, then phoned home to tell them the news.

And now I am trying to utilize the final piece of information she left me. *In desperation*, the notes say, *you can call me and I will come*. This is followed by a list of instructions. They're not complicated, not the way she said they were, or even frightening, but I hesitate. I'm used to the gift, it comes from within me, but this conjuring is what Carrick Jones would disparagingly refer to as hocus-pocus. And despite my years of dealing with the gift, I'm kind of on his wavelength about the whole hocus-pocus thing.

Still, I don't think I have any choice. I need advice and the only person who can give it to me is dead. What else can I do?

I settle myself deeper into the window seat and begin. I hold Mama Amata's broom in my left hand. I wear a bracelet woven from my hair and a crystal of rose quartz. I've surrounded myself with herbs: anise, bay laurel, camomile, thyme and saffron. I've taken a couple of valerian tablets.

There are other herbs on the list—betony, heliotrope, mortwort, jasmine, myrrh—but I don't have any of them in my house and can't get them at six o'clock on a Sunday morning. The ones around me are from my spice rack; the valerian from my medicine cabinet. They're probably past their sell-by dates, but I suspect it's the intention rather than the herbs themselves. At least I'm hoping that's true.

Because I have plenty of intention. I am desperate to talk to Mama Amata. She will know how I can convince Carrick Jones to work with me. She will know how to convince him that my gift is real, that I'm not a fake, that I can help him with Morrison's death. She will help me, finally, to save someone.

I place some of the herbs in a bowl and set a match to them. They're dry and the flame catches quickly, flaring for a moment, then settling into a steady rolling of scented smoke. The smell makes me hungry but I push that thought away and concentrate on the broom in my hand and the pages on the seat beside me.

I still hear Mom and Aunt Lucy, still smell the herbs, but suddenly, I know that if I open my eyes I will be able to see, even through the bandages. And I can. I open my eyes and see the room around me filled with a soft light. Through the window, I see the sun red in the sky and the trees, green and motionless and frighteningly still.

And I see shadows in the room, silent and chill

as death. Nothing moves, as if I have been transported into a painting which hung on the wall for generations, never changing, never moving. I'm part of that painting, and I wait for the door to open. The mandolin to play. The dog to gambol. Or the light to shift to the right.

None of this happens. I can't blink. The bandages have sealed my eyes but I see everything, all at once, without even a microsecond missing. Yet somehow I miss her arrival.

Because she's there, sitting in the chair across from me, her feet tucked up under her, her hands resting in her lap. She looks no different than she did the first day I saw her.

"Mama?"

"Ria. You are strong now, my child." She smiles at me. "But we have little time. Listen carefully. I will tell you what I can."

I open my mouth to tell Mama Amata why I need her advice but she stops me with a gesture.

"I know what you need," she says. "Do not speak, angel, just listen.

"Your inability to see the world has triggered the expansion of your powers." She holds up her hand again. "Yes, I know about last Friday night. Once I am gone, ask your mother or Lucy or even Carrick

Jones if any of them has experienced this type of feeling. At least one of them will say yes. This happens to many people, a feeling that something is going to happen and then it does.

"But what has occurred, what you have been able to do today, is quite different. You have chosen to consciously tap into your gift to get me here. This is something you have never done before. Your gift has always been triggered by something outside yourself, by a photograph. Now you will be able to access it whenever you concentrate on it."

"Will I be able to see further into the future? Will I…?"

I'm scared to ask the question I want answered.

Mama Amata smiles but it doesn't quite reach her eyes. I realize she no more knows this particular answer than I do.

"No one knows how far your gift will allow you to see but it is certain that it has changed, becoming stronger and, perhaps, more accurate. Only time and experimentation will show you the extent of the change."

I ponder her words for a moment. She is beginning to fade at the edges and I quickly put away my concerns for another time. Because another thing I am sure of is that this is the last time I'll see her.

"Thanks," I say, unable to articulate any of the other thoughts roiling around in my brain.

"I miss you," I say.

"And I miss you, my child."

She reaches for me but before our hands can meet, she is gone.

Warm hands are lifting me from the floor when I come back to myself. Their hands are trembling but I feel secure in them, even though I sense their fear.

"I'm fine, you two, really. I think it was just a little too much for the first time, concentrating that hard."

"What was it like?" Mom asks.

"I think it was like being hypnotized. Remember when we saw Raveen and he called you up to the stage?" I can't see her, of course, but I know she's nodding.

"It was probably just the same as that. All the time I could hear the two of you in the kitchen but I was totally focussed on something else."

"Mama Amata?" Aunt Lucy says the name in a whisper and with reverence, as if she were speaking in an empty cathedral. I almost hear the echoes.

"Hmmmm," I whisper back, "but I can't talk about it right now." I touch my hand to my throat and cough. "Tea, please, and lots of honey."

I'm not sure I've learned anything from my experience except that I could summon Mama Amata. Mom and Aunt Lucy are far more convinced than I.

Over the next twenty-four hours, the three of us come up with a plan—a series of experiments to test the extent of my gift—and Mom and Aunt Lucy insist on being there when I try it out. It'll take a while to see whether or not it works, but I'm not doing anything else. And I need the distraction.

The experiments begin with the Yellow Pages. I'm going to take them and run my fingers over the pages with photographs of real estate agents and lawyers and plumbers, anyone whose ad includes a photo. Mom or Aunt Lucy will write down the ones where I stop, where I think I feel something. We'll watch the news. Okay, I'll listen while they watch, and they'll read the obits to see if any of the names show up.

Mom is going to deliver a note to Carrick Jones with the names on it. He's not going to be happy if any of them die over the next week but tough, he's part of it whether he wants to be or not. On the other hand, maybe he will be happy—I'll be back on his list of suspects.

Three names stop me when I touch the pages from the phone book. I don't know any of them and neither do Mom or Aunt Lucy. They're strangers to us, which makes it better, especially for the purpose of Jones. There will be no reason for me to have anything to do with the deaths of these people.

It sounds callous to be thinking this way, but I can't devise any other way to figure out what my gift will do and how it will do it. I don't believe this will work but I can think of nothing else, except…

I'm going to get Mom to call and ask Carrick to bring me back the picture of Lisa. I haven't heard anything about her on the radio except that the police are still looking and they have no suspects, no idea at all, really, though of course they don't say that.

Hers is the only photograph I can think of that will give me this kind of focus. I know she's lost, missing, and I know from the way she looks at her kids and husband in the photo Carrick showed me that she loves them. She wouldn't leave them.

If Lisa is a kidnapping victim, she might be close to death. Or she will have died very recently. Maybe I can somehow channel my gift to see a recent death? Although when I think about actually doing that, I realize I have absolutely no idea how to go about it.

All of these ideas are easier thought about than done. Nothing happens. And still nothing happens. No call or visit from Carrick Jones. No one whose name I picked out of the Yellow Pages dies, at least that we can tell.

I'm starting to panic. There is nothing I can do while blind except think and all I can think about is Carrick Jones. This is not helping.

"Gran?" She's on shift with me during the day while Mom and Aunt Lucy are at work. "Can you drive me to the police station?"

I must be either crazy or desperate to ask her to drive. She's not only deaf, she's almost as blind as I am. She shouldn't be driving at all, but I console myself with the thought that if she shows up at the police station and backs into a cop car while she's trying to park, maybe they'll take away her license.

The other thing that makes the idea of a trip in Gran's car bearable is that I won't be able to see what's coming.

She suggests we phone first to make sure he's on duty. She does. He is.

The drive is scary, more frightening than if I'd been able to see. I hear brakes screeching, horns blaring. I feel the power stops—the only kind Gran knows how to make anymore. I swear I can feel the whoosh of the cars and buses missing us by six inches when they have to pass us on the right to stop themselves from plowing into us when she stops in the middle of the street. But no one hits us, and she, even when parking, doesn't hit anyone else, not even the tiniest bump.

It's a miracle.

The stairs up to the front door of the police station are steeper than I remember them, and longer. Gran's hand on my arm trembles as we finally reach the top of them and she holds open the door for me to pass through.

"Do you want me to wait with you?" she asks, concern clear in her loud voice.

"I'm fine," I say, though I'm not. "Just take me to the desk."

She guides me over to the desk. "I'll be here when you're done."

I point my face towards where I think the desk is. "I need to speak to Detective Jones. It's important."

A woman's voice. "Is he expecting you?"

"No, but he'll see me. My name is Ria Sterling."

I wait for an intake of breath to tell me she's recognized my name but I hear nothing. It's weird; last week I was a murder suspect and now she doesn't even know my name.

"I'll let him know you're here. Just…"

She wants to tell me to sit down and wait, but to do that she'll have to get up from behind her desk and lead me to a chair somewhere. I have power in this room. Being obviously blind—the bandages over my eyes are a dead giveaway—gives me the advantage. Carrick won't leave me standing here for long.

"Ms. Sterling?" An unfamiliar voice, but definitely male. "Detective Jones is busy right now. Maybe I can help you?"

Nice try, I think, but it's not going to work.

"No, thank you. I need to see Detective Jones. I'll just wait here until he's free."

I don't move and no one offers to bring me a chair or lead me over to the waiting area. Gran has disappeared from my hearing.

It's hard to tell how much time passes but the station is quiet around me so it's probably lunchtime when I hear his footsteps coming towards me.

He grabs my arm without saying a word and begins to lead me back out of the station. I dig my heels in and say, "Whoa, buddy, where are we going?"

"I don't want to talk to you. I know one of those women had to drive you down here so we're going to find her, and she's going to take you home."

"No."

He stops and I bang into him.

"Gran's left." I raise my voice so she can hear me from around the corner. "She's gone to do some errands. And no, she doesn't have a cell phone." By the end, I'm practically shouting.

Gran's great at taking hints, but she doesn't hear very well. I tug on Carrick's arm to distract him.

"You'll have to take me home."

I hear a deep sigh and heat starts to rise from his body. He's so pissed off he can't speak.

"Carrick?" I whisper. "Please. I really need to talk to you."

"Damn it, Ria. I don't want to talk to you about this. Can't you just leave it? Leave me alone? My partner's been murdered and I don't have a single fucking clue why. Lisa Martin is still missing and her husband is tight with the mayor—both of them are on my case every single day. It's enough, okay?

"I'll take you home and you'll stay there."

He pulls me behind him, muttering, "steps here," "turn left," "curb."

It's only when he puts his hand on my head to push me into the car that I feel any emotion other than anger from him. It's as if touching me calms him and he's able to reach past the anger and locate his desire for me. His touch gentles and his voice deepens.

"Ria, get in the car. I'll take you home."

I wait until his breathing has settled into my rhythm before I say anything. "Did you bring Lisa Martin's photograph?"

No answer.

"I think I might be able to tell you something now. Things have changed. I've changed." I speak slowly and say as little as possible.

"I don't know, Ria. It's not that easy, not now. The Chief pulled me off Morrison's murder and Lisa Martin's been missing for too long. No one expects her to be alive."

The sadness in his voice is overwhelming. If I could, I'd walk away and let him get on with it without any interference from me. It's obvious that I'm making his life more complicated.

"Just let me see the photograph. That's all. What can it hurt?"

I can feel the presence of the photograph, he's got it in his right jacket pocket so it's only a few inches from me. It's calling to me. Another thing that's never happened before. I'm kind of getting used to new experiences—I can't think of how many have occurred in the past couple of weeks.

"Stop. Stop. Right now. Damn it, Carrick, stop the car."

He doesn't hesitate, just stops the car. I open the door but don't get out.

"Where are we?"

"We're at Oakand 12th, right in front of Mc-Carron's."

I don't want to believe it and I know Carrick Jones is not going to be understanding but this is it.

"Did you bring the envelope Mom dropped off at the station?" For a moment I wonder why I can't feel that and I can feel Lisa's photograph but I can't imagine why he would come out without it. "Open it."

He sighs and I hear the rip of the paper.

I know what it says, Mom read it to me after she'd written it.

"Ria is experimenting with her gift. These three names are names she picked at random from pictures in the Yellow Pages. She sees that they will die soon." She dated the note and she and Aunt Lucy signed it. It's sealed inside two envelopes, one inside the other, with their initials across both flaps.

The three names were Josephine Fairley, florist; Patrick Anthony Xavier King, plumber; and Louise Ng, real estate agent. I didn't know any of them, neither did Mom or Aunt Lucy. They were, as far as we could tell, complete strangers. As fair a test as possible under the circumstances.

"Go inside, and check the bulletin board to see whose viewing is tonight."

Either he'll see one of the names and believe me, or he won't.

The engine ticks as it cools, my watch ticks, and

my brain goes with it. Tick. Tick. Tick. Since the bandages, I am completely incapable of figuring out time. I'm not even sure why I'm wearing my watch, but forever must be how long I wait before the footsteps reach the car and the door opens.

The ignition catches and we pull out into the street. I am not going to be the one to speak first. I'm not.

CHAPTER 9

I can't help myself.

"Carrick? What did you see?"

"Damn you, Ria Sterling," he whispers.

He's seen one of the names on the list.

"Damn you to hell, you witch."

He jams the car into gear and takes off, wheels spinning. He's breathing heavily, the car is lurching side to side as he takes the corners too fast, and I'm scared. Not of him, but for him. For us.

"What did you see?"

I peer across the car, straining to see something, anything, but of course I see nothing, no light, not even the shadow of something. I know the sun shines only because it's hot on my arm.

He doesn't answer me. But, as always, I feel his heart beating. It's fast, and irregular. I worry about a heart attack and gather my wits to tell him to relax.

"Slow down, Carrick, okay?"

I've forgotten to notice that my heart is pounding as quickly as his.

The tires still squeal as the car races around corners. I smell the brake pads burning as the seat belt tightens around my waist and chest. Carrick has slammed on the brakes, obviously just a little too late, and the swearing from the car across from us is loud enough to penetrate even the silence that seems to be surrounding us, enfolding us in a cone of silence, just like *Get Smart*.

I wait for the car to move again but it doesn't. Carrick's heart slows, as does mine.

"Do you want me to drive?" I ask this question seriously, prepared, if necessary, to rip off the bandages and maybe ruin my eyes for good. Because right now I don't care, I want to see Carrick's face. His voice, his heartbeat, his breathing, are no longer enough.

But he laughs. And the cone of silence lifts itself off the car.

"No, I don't want you to drive. Though could be you'd do a better job than I've been doing, huh?"

His hand lightly touches mine and then we're moving again.

"What did you see?"

"Josephine Fairley is being buried at Castle View tomorrow afternoon."

"Oh," a deep sigh escapes me. I'm not sure whether what I feel is relief or regret but, mostly, I'm just glad he's talking.

"When did she die?"

"Just two days ago."

"How?"

"The bulletin board doesn't tell you that, Ria. When was the last time you were at a funeral home? It only tells you that she's being buried tomorrow and the viewing is tonight."

I haven't been to a funeral home ever. The one time I wished I could have gone, I was in hospital, crying and crying and crying. Crying until I made myself so sick…

"Was her family…?"

I don't know what it is I want to ask but I do know I feel responsible for this death in a way I never have since I was fifteen and Mama Amata taught me to honor the gift, not hate it.

All the deaths foretold, all the pain caused, none of it avoidable. But this might have been. I should have told her, too, not just Carrick.

I don't want this. I don't want my gift. For the first time in years, I hate myself and my gift. I hate Mama Amata for saving me.

I have wanted to give it up, the way it complicates

my life, sets me apart from everyone else. I have wanted to be ordinary, a regular woman who could spend her weekends in the garden, or shopping for antiques, or dating.

I can't remember the last time I had a date. Nor the last time I did anything other than work. Monday to Friday at some job site, my hair and my body dripping with sweat, my face covered by a mask. Nights and weekends, well, it was obvious what I did then.

The note to Carrick is dated just a couple of days ago. She could have stopped driving, or swimming, or crossing streets. She could have saved herself. I could have saved her.

"I knew she was going to die. I knew where to find her and I did nothing to stop it. Oh my God, Carrick."

"Ria, you couldn't have stopped this."

"But… But… But…"

I can't get the words out.

"You couldn't have stopped it. First of all, there's no way she'd believe you. I didn't, and I had evidence."

The darkness is back in his voice, replacing the red anger that had returned to the car with him from the funeral home. He's thinking of Frank.

"Second, what would you have said to her? Don't do what?

"Don't go outside? She could have died in the bath. Or in a home invasion.

"Don't drive your car? She could have got hit at a crosswalk or by a bus.

"Don't go swimming? She might have died of a heart attack or liver cancer or... I can't think of enough diseases to prove this to you."

I know he's right. At least my brain knows he's right. But my heart and my body are not listening.

The hiccupping has started and now I'm frantic. What if I can't stop crying?

"Stop it. You can't change what's already happened."

"You're a fine one to talk," I say through my hiccups.

"Yup, I am. Because I live with regrets every single day of my life. So I know how you feel, and I know you'll only make yourself sick."

He can't know, I remind myself, *he can't know that I can make myself sick unto death.*

We both listen to me hiccupping for a while.

"Here."

There's a rustling on the seat beside me, the tap of a tab being opened, then a big warm hand wraps mine around a pop can.

"Drink this."

"You sound like someone in *Alice in Wonderland*."

"That's me. Now drink it and stop the hiccupping."

It doesn't stop the hiccupping but the lukewarm bubbles and serious sugar rush—no diet soda for Carrick Jones—calm me enough that I can stop sobbing between gulps.

"I'm taking you home. I'll tell this story only once. Are your family at your house?"

"No. You'll have to take me to my real home, instead."

I tell him the address and sit back, sipping the soda, and try to stop the hiccups. I drink backwards and I even contemplate telling Jones to start driving like a maniac again so I'll be scared out of my hiccups, but I resist that temptation. Frantic I may be, but stupid I'm not.

He helps me out of the car and up the sidewalk to the front porch. The door is unlocked and I open it as if I can see. I realize what I should have known for a week. I should be staying here. In this house, I am never blind, not since I was fifteen.

"Mom? Aunt Lucy? Gran? We need to talk to you."

The ice cubes in the tea ting gently against each other and the sun hits the left side of my body. I feel the heat and the tension in the room, and I know the hiccups have my family as scared as they have me. At least I've stopped the uncontrollable sobbing.

"Carrick?" That's my mother, incapable of patience when it comes to me. "What's going on?"

A shadow of a movement passes across my blind eyes and I realize that of the four people in the kitchen with me, the one to whom I am most closely attuned is not a member of my family, but Carrick Jones. I don't need to see him to know he's raised his hand for silence, nor that his face is sombre in the sunlight.

I see his chest rise and fall with each breath, see the dust motes outlining his hair, his lips pursing as he thinks about where to begin, how much to tell, how much of himself will need to be revealed in the telling.

"I was driving Ria home, and she told me to stop right in the middle of a street. We were in front of McCarron's."

His voice has dropped to a husky whisper. Part of me wants to reach across the table for his hand but the sensible part of me wins out. He has to tell this story.

"Ria told me to go in and see if one of the three names was on the bulletin board. Josephine Fairley died two days ago."

Mom and Aunt Lucy and Gran say nothing. I don't hear a surprised or shocked or frightened intake of breath from any of them. Even more than me, I realize, they have been expecting this.

Their faith in me is both frightening and satisfying. Right now it's mostly frightening.

"How did she know that Josephine Fairley was going to die? She couldn't see her photograph."

I feel him look at me, his perplexity as clear as a winter night when the snow crunches under your feet and it's so cold you can't tell any longer that the air chills you. The kind of night when you can die without seeing it coming.

"She sent me that letter after she was blinded. How did she do it?"

Mom says, "I don't know. *We* don't know. We think it's because she can't rely on sight anymore but her gift insists on manifesting itself. She can't see, but the gift is still there, waiting for her to open herself to it." She laughs, a sweet tinkle.

"I know this sounds ridiculous, but we can't think of any other explanation."

Aunt Lucy chimes in. "Something's changed, a fundamental shift in the way Ria sees the world, and the death within it."

"Okay, I'll give you the different manifestation of the gift, but I thought she only saw death a very short time before it happened."

"She does. It was only a couple of days."

I know it's time for me to speak but it's hard

through the hiccups. I listen to their breathing, waiting for that slight intake that signals talk, but it doesn't come and it's my turn.

"I think it's a combination of things."

I don't tell him that the reason I am so desperate is Carrick. The certainty that we must work together pulls at me all the time. But insisting on this will just put him off. And he doesn't ask, probably for the same reason.

Gran says, "I think it's your age, too, honey."

"My age?"

"Mmmmm. Women change, we all change, and it happens in cycles. I suspect you're right at the beginning of the middle one. Midlife-passage time."

Gran's an avid reader of self-help books and I wonder which guru-of-the-week has sold her on this theory.

"That makes sense," Carrick Jones say.

I almost fall out of my chair. *That makes sense*, he says? What in the hell does that mean?

"It happened to me, sort of," he says. "A few years ago I started feeling restless, unsettled, disgruntled. Couldn't figure out why. Started getting shaky, too. Scared of flying, scared of everything, really, except my job.

"Frank lived with my fears for a while, but it was

coming up time for our yearly weekend in Las Vegas.
I kept putting him off, wouldn't tell him why, but it
was because I couldn't for the life of me get on a plane.

"He made me tell him what was wrong, and then
he laughed." Carrick's joy in the memory shows up
as a clear yellow light.

"He made me see his psychiatrist. I hadn't even
known he had one. I pretty much walked in the door,
talked for five minutes, and he said, *midlife passage*.

"We get to a point in our life where we can see
the end, and we have to make decisions about who
we're going to be for the second half of our lives. I
still don't know that answer, but at least I understand
the feeling."

The three women murmur in agreement. I'm not
sure what to say or do, so I wait until the soft sounds
die away and then go back to finish off my list.

"Figuring out a way to see Mama Amata and
actually doing it.

"Beginning to believe in magic, not just the gift,
but the magic that's all around us."

And though I won't admit it, not yet, I think
Gran and Carrick Jones might be right. There is
something changing within me. And it's not just
about Carrick Jones.

"Look what happened with Josephine Fairley."

I don't mention the other two names—Patrick Anthony Xavier King and Louise Ng—though I know I'm going to have to remind Jones. I know they're dead, too, and I suspect he does as well.

"Let's get to work."

These are the last words I expect to hear from Carrick Jones. His voice is calm and strong but beneath it I still sense his disbelief. I see the tiny quaver of uncertainty as a wavery line through the words, and know that he's going to work with me as a way of hedging his bets.

Despite the evidence, he doesn't believe.

CHAPTER 10

Mom and Aunt Lucy, Gran and Carrick Jones discuss the terms of my retainer while I try and ignore the hurt running through me. It doesn't take long before the hurt amps itself up into anger. I'm furious.

If Carrick's aura is yellow, mine is red. I can't see it in the same way as I see his, but I feel it, heating me up like I'm sitting under a sun lamp, the kind that gives you skin cancer. I'm surprised no one else feels the anger rolling off me.

"I'm outta here. You guys decide what you want me to do and when. Give me a call at home."

I pick up the phone, touch dial a cab, and head for the front door. I figure if I move fast enough, no one will stop me.

The women understand why I'm leaving and they don't question or try to stop me. I know they have their hands on Jones, restraining him.

Aunt Lucy says, "Call when you get home, okay?"

"Of course."

On the way home in the cab, I imagine the conversation going on around the kitchen table.

Aunt Lucy: *She just needs some time alone.*

Gran: *Bullshit. She's pissed off with Jones here. It's obvious.*

Jones: *Why? What did I do?*

Mom: *More what you didn't do. You have your evidence—Josephine Fairley—but you still don't believe in her.*

Jones: *Of course I do. I want to work with her.*

And there my imagination breaks down.

I lock the doors behind me and feed Fatcat, ignoring the shrill ring of the phone. It sounds as angry as I actually am.

The house feels cold and I realize I've forgotten to ask Jones if he's found the guy at the job site. I sit down at the kitchen table with a glass of wine, memorizing a list of things I have to do in the morning:

Call Marathon to see if I still have a job.

Check with my insurance agent and the union about my disability.

Give Aunt Lucy a list of groceries I need.

Ask her to come over and check my mail.

Send Fatcat with her for his shots. They deserve each other.

Call the gardener and ask him to keep coming.

Call Jones about the prank at the job site.

Tell him I've changed my mind about working with him.

Bang. Bang. Bang. The wine glass rattles on the table.

"Open up, Ria. It's me."

I ignore him.

Bang. Bang. Bang. The screen door screeches as Carrick tries to open it.

He sounds exactly like a brutal cop on TV. "Open the goddamned door, Ria." He rattles the handle.

I sip my wine and wait. He'll go away eventually. He doesn't want me enough to persist with this banging. He's got some bug in his mind about it, but it's a weak one.

"Now, Ria. Open the door right this minute or I'll break the window."

Fatcat's at my feet. He's trembling. I'm not. Carrick Jones may be angry but he isn't going to hurt me. I hold up the phone in my hand and mime dialling 9-1-1.

"Calling the cops? Go ahead. I'm coming in."

He can't get in through the kitchen window, it's too small. He'll back off. The glass shatters in the porcelain sink.

"Watch out for my plants." It's all I can think of to say.

Muffled swearing as he pulls himself through the window, a couple of plant pots falling into the sink with him. I hand him the Dustbuster.

"Clean up your mess before you say a single word to me. And stop breaking in here and scaring Fatcat."

The cat comment is obviously a non-starter. Fatcat has left the under-table comfort and is purring madly somewhere in the vicinity of the broken window.

Being blind seems to have lost me the advantage of silence. Because I can't see his eyes, I can't tell what he's thinking, whether he's just ready to say something or he's got enough patience to wait me out. Being blind also seems to have cost me any patience I did have.

"I'm glad you're here," I choose to say. "Have you found out anything about the guy at the job site?"

The table settles as he leans against it. I can't help thinking of his big gorgeous body but I don't care. He's just another movie star to me—I can replace my Carrick Jones fantasy with Johnny Depp or Jude Law or Hugh Jackman. I have about the same chance with them as I do with Jones.

"He didn't work for Marathon. They're sure of that."

"God, Jones, don't be naïve. They're so stupid they

think the fewer workers they have the more money they're making. How in the hell do you think they're going to be able to keep track of transient workers?"

"They say they don't have any. They say they hire a crew at the beginning of the job and they never replace anyone who leaves. They say everyone on the site has been there since the beginning and everyone was in sight of someone else that afternoon. In fact, they say, except for the foreman and a couple of odd-job guys putting away some tools, everyone except you had left.

"And what in the hell were you doing up there by yourself at that time of the night? You're not gifted, you're crazy."

I want to tell him that the two things often go hand in hand. I want to tell him the stories Mama Amata told me of people she knew who'd gone crazy because they couldn't deal with their gifts, locked up for life, hearing voices, seeing things. They can't be cured because they aren't sick, but the institutions and the doctors don't understand that.

You have to learn to deal with your gift, Ria. If not, you will die. Or you will go crazy. There are no other choices.

Mama Amata's voice saying those words is burned into my memory. It's my mantra on days when I'm losing it.

"We were falling behind, and I kept losing help-ers. They got fired or quit or just didn't show up. I wanted to finish off one thing. Besides, I'm used to dealing with those men. I felt safe."

I shiver a little. What if I never feel safe at a job site again? It's the only thing I know how to do. And I love it. Welding satisfies me. It's neat, efficient and beautiful. It pays me enough to have this house and feed Fatcat.

"But we can't find the guy. He had to have somehow got past the security, onto the site. Or Marathon is lying to me. No one saw anyone who didn't belong, so he's good. There were enough workers on their way out that someone should have seen him."

"Maybe they're hiding it because they don't like me. Maybe they were all in on it."

"Paranoid, much? Listen, I interviewed every single person who worked on that job site. They might not have liked you but every man jack of them said they were sorry you were hurt. They even sent you flowers."

The chair next to me squeaks as Carrick Jones lowers himself into it and asks, "You want a cup of tea? Or a beer?"

"A beer, please. They're in the fridge." The red wine is too sensual for this conversation.

The caps pop and the beer is cold and refreshing. I'm tempted to press Jones on the man, but the answer I'll get is something I don't want to hear.

"Ria?" His voice is soft. "Someone meant to hurt you. Who do you think might want to do that?"

"Pissed-off cops? Out-of-work welders? I've never noticed anyone hating me enough to want to hurt me. There's no way they could have known my blindness would be temporary. It could just as easily have been permanent."

Might still be, I think, not wanting to give those words their full effect by speaking them out loud.

"But someone did." Just like a cop, having to speak the obvious.

"Yeah, okay, someone did. But I still think it was an accident."

"It wasn't an accident and we need to figure out who it was and why. It has be about your *gift*." As always, he puts verbal quotation marks around that word.

"I don't think so, but even if it was about my *gift*, we have no way of figuring out who it might have been. I've seen hundreds of people in the last fifteen years and I don't remember more than a dozen of them well enough to find them again." I do have a record, but it's incomplete, and this isn't the time to mention it. I just want him gone.

"We'll start there."

I think of the sad, lonely and scared people I've seen over the years, most of them women, but dozens of men as well. And I know—because of the past days—that there must be someone among them who might harm me, but I can't think of who it would be. I can't think of *why* it would be. I don't do any harm to anyone.

I let my mind drift back over the years. I can't remember everyone, not even most of them, but I'm trying to see if there is someone who stands out, someone who feels wrong.

"There must be someone," I say to Carrick, "but…"

He nods and waits. Cop waiting. Cop patience. I try harder to think of a man who worried me at the time, but I can't.

I shake my head wearily. "There must be someone, but I can't do this tonight." I take a deep breath, then another.

"We're not going to work together," I say. "It's just going to make things worse."

Without warning, a headache hits me with the force of a typhoon. I can't breathe through the pain and I can't speak.

"Ria? Ria?"

Hands pull me up from the chair and place me on

the cold kitchen floor. My feet are placed on the chair and my arms pulled above my head.

"Breathe. In. Out. In. Out."

I don't know what brings the breath back to my body—the touch of Carrick Jones, the physical realignment, the voice in my ear repeating, "Breathe. In. Out. In. Out." But whatever it is, it works.

And I know why it happened, too. It's the damned gift warning me, *use me or lose more than just the gift*. I got more than I bargained for when I chose to start down this path. Because it's never been this strong before, never been able to affect anything in the real world.

I'm desperate to distract Carrick from my gift but the only distraction I can think of is really stupid. I try it anyway.

"What's the best book about being a detective? Not a fiction book, I mean, but the book detectives study from. You know, that big fat book on everything you ever wanted to know about being a cop. Like that one."

I point toward the big grey book with red titles that lives on the counter next to the microwave— *Modern Welding*—the welder's bible. Tells you everything you'd ever need to know about every kind of welding, all in one handy five-pound volume. Even has pictures of white guys dressed in clothes from the 50s, unchanged since the first edition.

"There isn't a book, Ria. I did a degree in criminology, went to police college, studied for years to pass my detective's exam. But none of that meant anything. I learned everything I know about being a cop from Frank."

"Okay, that worked for you, but there must be a book. What did you use in college?"

"Ria, you don't need a book because you aren't going to have anything to do with this investigation. Neither am I. I'm off Frank's murder and I'm sidelined on the Lisa Martin case. The chief thinks I'm too close to both things, thinks I need to get on with my life. He's handed them over to someone else."

Whatever I might think I know about this man, whatever I might imagine about him, there is one thing I know with absolute certainty. Carrick Jones will not be sidelined. He will keep looking for Frank's killer. He'll keep looking for Lisa Martin.

I have another flash of inspiration. This time, the headache is manageable. Instead of piercing, it settles down to a dull roar behind my sightless eyes.

"Carrick? Let me up."

I push his hands away and scramble to my feet. I sit back down in my chair and finish my beer, silently holding out the empty can as an indication of my need for another.

I'm surprised when Carrick obliges, placing a cold can in my hand, then sitting back down at the table opposite me.

I hear him sip and imagine his hands cradling the cool container. I picture him leaning back in the chair and gradually relaxing, his eyes closing, the lines around his beautifully shaped lips and between his brows disappearing.

For the first time since I've met him, Carrick Jones is calm. And I'm going to have to spoil it.

Or do I? Maybe my flash of inspiration can wait. Maybe what I think I know is stupid—like telling Jones that I think Frank knew something he didn't about the killer.

Because this is all new to me, I'm hesitant, especially after Carrick's all-too-obvious disbelief earlier, to believe in it. Just because I get a headache doesn't mean the flashes are real.

"Headaches are a natural part of recovery," I say out loud, repeating the words of the doctor. "But if they persist, or get worse, come back in to see me."

"Ria? Do you have a headache?"

I turn my head toward his voice and hope he can read the snarky expression on my face.

"Yes," I snap. "I have a bitch of a headache. And no," I anticipate his next question, "I don't want to go the hospital. I want you to go away."

And suddenly more than anything, I want to crawl upstairs to bed. I need some sleep. I don't care if it's the middle of the day or the middle of the night. I can't tell the difference and my body needs some downtime.

I push back from the table.

"Off you go." I flap my hands at him. "Lock the door behind you."

Not that the door matters since he broke the kitchen window. But I don't care. I just want him gone.

He says nothing but I sense his nod. When he speaks, he shows more tact than I'd given him credit for.

"I'll call your mom and get her to come over. I'll call the glazier to fix the window."

I can't talk, can barely shuffle my way out of the kitchen.

I'm not surprised when Carrick pulls me from my shaky feet and into his arms. I'm not surprised, I'm thrilled at the feel of his arms around me and at the steady beat of his heart against my chest.

He smells good and I give myself permission to relax into the aroma of Carrick Jones. I can't define it, even with my heightened sense of smell, but it's inescapably Jones. Definitely not sweet, but a hint of some exotic spice under a male idea of soap and shampoo. I bet he doesn't even know he wears this scent.

I wonder if anyone else has noticed it, wonder if it's really there or if it's something that's part of the way I smell Carrick. Maybe it's just how I *want* him to smell.

Because if he has that exotic side to him, he'll eventually come to understand and accept my exotic side. My *gift*.

I grin, forgetting for a moment that just because I can't see him doesn't mean he can't see me.

"What's so funny?"

His voice rumbles against me. I laugh, out loud this time.

"Nothing. Really," I say. "It's nice, though, being carried up to my bedroom."

I know that the rest of that sentence, though unspoken, hovers in the air between us. In big red-hot passionate letters. And I know he sees it by the catch in his breath. So I say it.

"I want you, Carrick Jones."

CHAPTER 11

The rest of the trip up the stairs is accomplished in complete silence, except for the creak of the old treads, the light susurration of our breathing, and my barely suppressed giggles.

I love shocking Carrick Jones and even more, I love his reaction—an unrestrained hiss and an almost imperceptible moan, accompanied, I bet, by ever more increasing pressure on his zipper.

Carrick gingerly opens the door at the stop of the stairs and I grin again. "Scared?" I ask him.

"Of what?"

His voice, deep to start with, has dropped an octave.

"Of me," I reply, resisting his attempts to drop me on the bed. I snuggle further into his arms and wait for the perfect moment. It doesn't take long to arrive.

Carrick leans over the bed and tries to unhitch my arms from around his neck.

"Let go," he whispers, his voice as strained as I picture his jeans to be.

I pull him off balance and onto the bed with me, my arms still wrapped tightly around his neck. Even without sight, I see the struggle in his face.

He wants to stay and he knows—without a single doubt—that he should go. He knows because it's his job. He knows because I can't see. He knows because he's still uncomfortable, maybe even scared, about my gift.

I wait to see which side will win and while I do, I enjoy the weight of his body on mine. He's warm and alive and I need that feeling. It's been a long time since a man has been in my house, let alone my bedroom, and I'm going to savor every minute of it.

I know the very moment he makes his decision. His weight settles on me, as if he can't resist the feel of us together, and then he lifts himself onto his elbows. Carrick's exotic unbridled side has lost to his practical go-by-the-rules side.

Loosening but not releasing my grip around his neck, I offer him an option.

"Turn out the lights and close the blinds. There's nothing you can do tonight and no point in disturbing Mom when you can stay with me."

I tighten my arms and lift myself until my lips are next to his right ear.

"Carrick," I whisper, teasing and serious at once, "just sleep with me, okay? I'd like the feel of your body in my bed." I pause. "Unless, of course, you can't resist me?"

My giggles can't be suppressed and it isn't long before Carrick's deep laugh joins me. I may not have won the battle, and the war is definitely ongoing, but this skirmish goes to me.

His warmth vanishes and I hear the click of the light switch, the tick-tick of the blinds dropping over the windows. I've already struggled out of my jeans and T-shirt, trying not to be too obvious about it.

The bed sinks.

"Stop," he says and hands me back my T-shirt. "Leave it on."

There is no give in his voice so I take the T-shirt. I know the room is pitch black so I don't waste any stretches on him.

"Now you," I say. "You can't sleep in your boots and jeans."

He's thinking about it. I can almost hear the wheels turning in his hard head and I laugh again. I've laughed more tonight than I have in weeks.

"Come on, Carrick. Take off your damn boots

and come to bed. You don't want me. I get it. I just want to sleep with you."

The dull roar is my reward. And the thump of his boots on the floor. My mouth dries at the sound of the zipper but I ignore my baser instincts—and raise the covers in invitation.

"I'm tired, Jones. And I haven't had a good night's sleep since I met you. You owe me."

He still hasn't said a word and, suddenly, it doesn't matter. His arms go around me and his long hard body fits against my back. I can't stop the sigh of satisfaction nor my body's automatic reaction. I snuggle further back, pushing my butt against his obviously willing penis.

I laugh one last time and say, "Thanks, Jones. This is beyond the call of duty."

"You're not kidding," and I hear both humor and desire in his voice.

The desire sets my body humming but it's the humor that pushes me over the edge. Carrick Jones is—and I see this with a clarity seldom given to me—the love of my life. And with that thought, and the strength of his arms around me, I slide into sleep.

Waking up is nowhere near as satisfying. I slept like the dead and honestly, that's exactly what it felt like. I don't often sleep without dreaming and when I do, it feels as if I've lost something, some finely wrought and fragile connection to the world around me.

It's odd, because I never remember my dreams, haven't ever, that I know of, remembered a single dream. Not in any detail, anyway. But they stay with me during the day—the emotion of them sticks.

If I'm sad or elated or frightened, I know that I've dreamt that feeling in the night. And no matter what kind of day I have, I can't shake the dream feeling. I know it's not my own because it's somehow layered just under *my* emotions.

It's like one of those fancy drinks you get in upscale bars. My emotions are the lightest of the alcohols, laying right on the surface—vodka or rum or gin—while the dream feelings are much heavier and thicker and they sink right to the bottom, crème de menthe or Bailey's Irish Cream.

But they don't mix together like the alcohols do when you tilt the glass to drink it. My feelings and the dream feelings stay separate—mine on top, the dream feelings on the bottom.

I can't ignore them, but over the years I have learned to separate them out—like chaff from wheat—and, if not exactly ignore them, at least avoid worrying about them.

Because one thing is perfectly clear to me about

my dreams and the feelings that come with them. They are, in some way I can't decipher, may never be able to decipher, directly related to my gift.

So a night without dreaming is not just unusual, it's frightening.

Add that fear to my blindness and the woman who sits up in bed is a complete mess. And she's alone.

"Carrick?" I raise my voice and hope—knowing that hope is a waste of time—that he's not gone. I can't feel his presence anymore. "Jones?"

Kicking the covers off and cursing him all the while, I carefully crawl out of bed, knowing I dropped my clothes somewhere on the floor in the excitement of last night.

"You know, Carrick Jones, you're an ass. A complete ass. And you're a jerk, an unreasonable uncaring jerk. And," I continue muttering as I reach the windows and haul on the blinds. "You have no idea, do you? You don't just leave a blind woman alone after your first night together. It's inconsiderate. It's rude. And," yanking at the stupid unmoving blinds with all my might, "you're more than an ass, more than a jerk, you're a…"

The blinds clatter to the floor, each separate blade hitting my hands and forearms as they drop from the window. I've ripped my specially made wooden blinds right off the window. And, from the feel of my arms and hands, acquired more than a few cuts in doing it.

The pain hasn't yet reached whatever part of my brain processes it, but I know it will. And soon. I back away from the window, feeling with my bare feet for the blinds and my clothes. I need to get to the phone on my bedside table.

I need my mother.

And as if by some miracle, the door to the bedroom opens and she's there.

"Ria?"

I hear the worry in her voice and the clicking of her heels as she crosses the floor to me.

"I came as soon as Carrick called," she says. And then she sees my arms. I know they're bad, it's clear in the abrupt intake of her breath and the sudden stillness in the room.

But my mother, even under the most difficult of circumstances, is always my mother. Serene, unflappable, resourceful.

"Where's your first aid kit?"

"Under the kitchen sink," I say, each word ripped from my throat because the pain has now very definitely reached my brain. My arms feel as if a thousand miniature toy soldiers with very tiny, very sharp swords have had a go at the only part of me they could reach.

Before she goes downstairs, Mom brings me cool wet towels and wraps them around my arms.

"I'll be right back," she says, patting me on the shoulder. "I'm sure it looks worse than it is."

And I am reassured by those words. Mom wouldn't say *sure* if she wasn't. At least, I don't think she would. But she isn't calling the paramedics. Not yet, anyway.

I concentrate on figuring out a way to get the blood out of my extremely expensive cream-colored bathroom towels when this is all over. I alternate that with trying to calculate, purely by feeling, the number of cuts I have and whether any of them need stitches.

It's a good thing this happened now, is my next thought. I'm already on disability and I suspect that the cuts and the blindness might heal right around the same time. Too far down the road for my peace of mind, but at least I won't be off work *and* not making any money.

I can think about all of these things because my mom is downstairs and she can fix anything, because the cool towels have toned down the pain just enough for relatively lucid thought.

Just as Mom comes back through the door, I remember the second flash of inspiration I had last night.

"Mom? I need to see Lisa Martin's picture again.

Call Jones. He can have someone drop it off this morning."

She says, "Okay," and then kneels by my side. The sharp smell of disinfectant combines with the lavender shampoo she uses and the faint aroma of Chanel No. 5. Mom always smells this way—although usually without the disinfectant.

She hands me a glass and puts two tablets into my other hand. "Take these. They'll help with the pain."

If I could still see, the next few minutes would be far worse, I know they would. It's not that I hate the sight of blood, it's only that it's my own.

Mom's gentle fingers touch the cuts, and I count out along with her touches.

"One. Two. Three." I lose track somewhere around twenty. "I'm not going to faint," I say.

She pats me on the shoulder again. "Do you want to take a break? I've finished with your right arm."

"How bad is it?"

"They're shallow. I think the bruising will be worse than the cuts. You're definitely going to want to wear long sleeves, maybe for a couple of weeks."

"Finish them up." I grit my teeth and start counting again. She's right though, each time she touches one of the cuts I feel a deeper, darker pain waiting beneath it. "Mom?"

"You know you don't have to ask, Ria. You and Fatcat can come home with me as soon as I've finished here."

"You'll phone Jones first."

It's not a question because it has to be done. I haven't handled her picture since that first day I met Jones and she's still missing. Maybe…

Maybe what? Maybe your gift has completely transformed itself and suddenly, after thirty years, you're going to be able to see the living?

It's not that, I tell myself, unwilling to articulate what it really is.

Maybe what, then?

Maybe she's dying right now.

And what will it help to know that?

Nothing. It won't help at all.

At this point, I desperately want to end this stupid conversation I'm having with myself but it helps to take my mind off what my mother is doing. I go back to the stupid conversation. It's better—slightly— than my imagination.

But I need to know. And, I think of this as my winning response, my gift has changed. I knew Josephine Fairley was going to die without even seeing her photograph. And that if Jones believes me and

Lisa Martin's not already dead, they'll redouble their efforts to find her.

I feel better for having articulated this flash of inspiration. At least I'll be doing something. And I'll have a reason to get in contact with that jerk Carrick Jones.

"What kind of man would leave a blind woman all alone?" I say it out loud though I'm pretty sure I don't mean to.

"What kind of man would phone that woman's mother and wait on the porch until she shows up?"

"The kind of man who's scared to face you."

"Yeah, and why's that?"

I can feel my mother's grin. She's very carefully not asking me about my sex life but I answer her anyway.

"Nothing," I say. "I tried. I think he's scared of me."

"Of your gift?"

Mom knows how I've avoided telling anyone I'm dating about my gift ever since Jack. As soon as he found out, he demanded his engagement ring back and I never saw him again.

"Partly," and then I'm more honest than I want to be, "maybe more than partly. He doesn't trust me because of Frank. But it's more than that. It's the whole idea of it. Not just me, but in general."

I wonder why—besides the basic cop belief in only what they can see—Carrick has this huge chip on his shoulder for anything that even slightly smacks of the occult. I've seen him sneer as we pass a New Age shop; listened to him snort in disbelief at horoscopes on the radio; even someone stepping over the cracks in the sidewalk or around a ladder or a black cat elicits a look of disgust.

Mom doesn't say anything further, just finishes wrapping the gauze over the slimy antibiotic cream she's smeared on my arm. If Carrick wasn't interested in me before, just wait until he sees me now. Arms and hands wrapped up like a mummy, unshowered, wearing yesterday's wrinkled clothes and smelling like a hospital emergency room.

"Mom. Go call Carrick. I need the photograph."

"I'm going. But don't move, okay? I don't want you tripping over something and getting slivers or breaking your nose."

"Go," I say. "This is important."

I breathe a sigh of relief as her footsteps fade away down the hallway. Now I can let the tears I've been holding back fall freely.

I'm not sure whether I'm crying more about the pain or about that jerk Carrick Jones but it doesn't matter. I only have a few minutes to get it all done and over with.

I don't want my mother to see me crying. She watched more than enough of that when I was a teenager.

CHAPTER 12

By the time she got through the maze of telephone lines at the station to get to Carrick, by the time she'd convinced him to send over the photograph, I'd managed to stop crying.

I try not to cry—in fact, I don't think I've shed tears more than a handful of times since I was a teenager. I don't cry in movies or when I'm reading, I don't cry when I've hit my thumb with a hammer or go to emergency to get stitches. Not even when I break a bone, which happens fairly regularly to anybody working construction.

Crying scares me. If I start, will I be able to stop? I'm never quite sure, so I have learned all sorts of ways to avoid starting.

Raise your eyes to the ceiling. It stops the tears.

Don't—ever—read the obits.

Don't rent movies which have the word *poignant*

on the cover. It's a synonym for tearjerker. The same goes for books.

Don't watch war movies, movies about kids or diseases.

Do not listen to the radio on Sundays.

Do not watch or listen to talk shows—someone invariably has to tell their tale of woe.

For only about the millionth time, I wonder again why it is that I can watch television. And movies, for that matter. I've probably seen dozens of people on the news who were just about to die but I've never known it.

I do have a theory, but I know it's not very scientific and likely to be completely indefensible. It might be that movies and television are filtered many times before I see them. They're filmed, then edited, then transferred to another medium to be shown, then shown on a movie or TV screen.

Photographs are taken, then reproduced. And most of the photos I see are exact copies of the originals (or they are the originals). Although, and this is where I know my theory collapses, it works with photos in books and in the newspaper and magazines, which must be filtered just as many times as TV or movies.

Anyway, back to my list of things I can and can't do if I want to avoid crying.

Do not read Dickens.

Do read Jane Austen.

So I have a list of rules and I follow them, but what happened last night and this morning was outside of all my guidelines.

What rule could I make to stop this happening again?

Don't fall for Carrick Jones?

Don't get angry enough at the jerk Carrick Jones that you pull your wooden blinds down on yourself?

Okay, maybe I'll include that rule in my list. I can probably follow that one, especially as I no longer have any blinds.

I add one more rule which doesn't relate directly to the crying thing but is probably the most crucial of all of them.

Try not to push Carrick Jones too far. You'll lose him if you do.

This rule, I know, I am incapable of following. There is something about this man, this moment in my life, that makes me impatient. I've learned more about my gift in the past few weeks, even managed to expand its scope, and for that reason alone I'll keep pushing.

And, although I don't want to admit it, Carrick Jones is the one man I want.

No way to get around either of these things, I tell myself, so I'll just have to live with the consequences, like them or not.

A shiver runs up my spine and my head turns automatically toward the door.

"That's not right," I whisper. I would have heard Mom coming up the stairs but she's still in the kitchen. I hear her heels on the linoleum.

But someone is watching me.

Since I've been wearing these damn bandages, I've been able to sense the presence of other people. Scent, maybe a slight displacement of the air in a room, almost imperceptible sounds. Whatever the reason, I know someone is watching me.

But I also know whoever it is, is not in my room.

So where is he? I don't know why I assume the watcher is male but it seems obvious to me, not even worth thinking about. So where is he?

Once I think more carefully about it, where he is is as obvious as his being male. He's on the hill out back. If I could see, I would be able to see the spark of light off his binoculars. Okay, he might have a telescope. Or, damn, a rifle scope. But both of those items would be pretty noticeable in my sweet little neighborhood on a Saturday morning. No, probably binoculars.

I don't move, don't want to give him any indication that I know he's there. I bring my hand up to my face and hide my mouth from his view.

"Mom," I call, loudly enough that she'll hear me from the kitchen. Her steps quicken, begin to climb the stairs.

"Stop right there," I yell as she hits the fourth step. "Don't come up."

I can almost hear the thoughts racing in her mind. *My baby's in trouble. I have to go to her.* Then, more slowly, *but she doesn't want me up there.*

She hesitates and I take advantage of her hesitation. "There's someone watching me from the hill out back."

And here is the real reason I love my mother. She doesn't question how her blind-for-now daughter can know this, doesn't run screaming up to my room to protect me.

Instead she asks, "Should I phone Carrick?"

Of course that's what she should do but I race around in my head for a few moments searching for a solution that doesn't involve him. There isn't one.

So I answer, "Yes," and continue. "Don't use the phone in the kitchen. He might be able to see you."

Thanks once more to Carrick Jones, who broke the window yesterday, the only window in the house

with those expensive blinds set in between two panes
of glass. Break the window, lose the window covering.
I'm suddenly even more angry at him than I was when
I realized he had left me alone this morning.

"Why don't you come downstairs?" The anxiety
in Mom's voice is clear.

"I want him to stay out there until Carrick sends
someone. I want to know who he is."

"Oh," she says and steps back down the stairs.
Calling Carrick twice in such a short time is so not
going to endear me to him but what else can be
done? This is all—except for the blindness—his
fault. If he and Frank had gone somewhere else on
that Friday night I would not be in this mess.

I still feel the man's presence but I seem to have
lost my ability to tell how long I've been sitting on
my bed. Five minutes? Half an hour? All I know is
that it seems like forever since I fell asleep with
Carrick's arms around me and woke to find him gone.

And now the presence is gone as well. Boots
thump on my porch and a heavy hand pounds at the
front door.

"Police."

Carrick. He really is an idiot. As if I, or my
mother, wouldn't open the door to him. Though
after his miserable stunt this morning, he might not

be so certain about me. I grin. The day just got way more interesting.

It's a good thing Carrick came himself, I realize as the rest of the police go out the back door toward the hill. Explaining my *feeling* to Carrick is hard enough.

I sit in the chair in the kitchen, drinking Mom's coffee, and pray that they will find some evidence of someone being on my hill.

Still warm cigarette butts, a copy of this morning's newspaper, a Starbucks cup with an inch of lukewarm Colombian in the bottom. Footprints, fingerprints—though on what I don't know, a thread caught on a twig, or a butt or knee print in the damp ground.

"Why would someone be watching you?" asks Carrick Jones, his voice carefully neutral.

"I don't know." But I can think of a bunch of reasons even if he can't. I add *lacks imagination* to my list of Carrick's bad traits. My mother saves me the necessity of answering Jones.

"Peeping Tom? A dissatisfied customer?"

I knew she would mention that. My family spends far more time than I do worrying about the possibility of a disgruntled customer showing up. I've tried to tell them that the people who come to me seek resolution. I'm their last, best hope and a slim one at that.

Because what are the chances that one of the missing will die right after they come to see me?

They must be astronomical.

But my gift somehow combines with the appearance of the relatives to produce a much higher number of deaths than should be possible.

It's not me but the person who comes to me with the photograph. I think many of the people who seek my gift feel something, a light touch somewhere in their mind or their heart that tells them that the person they love, the lost one, is in danger.

They come to me and, more times than could be predicted under any scheme of odds-making, I tell them news of their lost one. And the ones I do tell seem satisfied, not exactly content, but settled, as if knowing is better than not.

Mom continues with her list of possibilities.

"The man who blinded her?"

I feel a shiver of recognition at that question but have no idea what it means. Why would that man, someone who works with me—for that's who it had to be, despite Carrick's thoughts to the contrary on the matter—watch me from the hillside? What other connection could we have?

"What if," she says, stealing my thoughts, "there is a connection? Between Ria and your partner?

What if someone didn't want them to get together? The man who killed your partner? He might think that Ria knows something about him."

"Except she doesn't," Carrick gently reminds her. "She doesn't know anything about who killed Frank. No one does," his voice darkens, "at least not yet."

"Well, Carrick Jones," my mother's worry and anger color her next statement. "You got her into this, you damn well better get her out."

I smile in her direction and say, "He didn't get me into anything I haven't been in for most of my life." I twist around on my chair until I'm pretty sure I'm facing the window. "Are they still looking?"

"It'll probably take a while."

"Not as long as all that. There's only one place on the hill where you can see into my bedroom. I've checked it."

But of course they find nothing. I'm not surprised and neither, from the sound of it, is Carrick. When the rest of the police have left, and my mother has gone home to pick up Gran and go grocery shopping, I ask him.

"You didn't believe me, did you?"

He avoids answering the question. "We had five police officers up there checking things out."

"They didn't find anything?"

"There's no sign of anyone being up on that hill."
I hear what he doesn't say, *and I look like an idiot for listening to some blind witch*.

"There was someone up there."

"Yeah, sure."

He doesn't believe me but he was worried enough to take the risk of looking like a fool to make sure that I am wrong.

"No cigarette butts?"

"Please, no one smokes any more, and even if he did, with all the cop shows on TV he would know better than to smoke. Or, if he did, he'd take the butts with him."

I smile for the first time all morning. "Do you watch those shows?"

"Sometimes," and his voice has lightened just a bit.

"You watch them for the babes, huh? Not for the cop stuff."

He laughs and then says, "I have to go. But I don't want to leave you alone here."

"It's okay. Fatcat and I are moving over to Mom's house. Gran and Mom should be back in a few minutes to help me pack. Can you wait that long?"

He sighs and I imagine him looking at his watch, impatience on his face. "Okay, I'll wait."

We sit at the table, cold coffee in front of both of

us, and we wait. No words are spoken but the sorrow in the room builds until I can almost touch it. I'm grieving for Josephine Fairley, because I failed to save her, and Carrick is grieving for Frank Morrison, because he believes he failed to save his partner.

The back door opens just before I start to scream.

"You ready to go?" Gran asks.

"I am, I just have to pack." I turn to where I feel Carrick Jones, standing, waiting to run out of the house. "Give Gran the picture," I say. "The one of Lisa Martin. She'll call you if I feel anything."

I hear Carrick murmuring to Gran and then his footsteps fading as he hurries to the front door.

Now what?

CHAPTER 13

Because no matter how difficult our relationship is going to be, and it is going to be tough, we *need* to work together. Not just for me, but for Carrick as well.

We have to figure out a way to get past the guilt and responsibility we feel, the sorrow we can't seem to dispel, and get on with our lives. I, for one, don't want to live the rest of my life feeling as badly as I've done for the first part of it. And I definitely don't want Carrick to feel that pain every single day, either.

But I have no idea how I'm going to accomplish this and figure out how to use my gift. *And* figure out what's going on with Frank Morrison and Lisa Martin and the man who blinded me. Not to mention the man who has been watching me from the hillside.

At least that problem is solved.

If you can call running away solving a problem. This morning I'm moving home. I love my house, love its setting in the rolling hills on the edge of the town, the creaking wooden floors and the sense of solitude it gives me, but home for me is still the house I grew up in.

Home for me is my family.

They give me sanity. They believe in me, even when I don't believe in myself. And right now, more than anything else, I need that belief.

Because I've just realized, sitting here in the car waiting for Mom to clean out the fridge so the food that's there doesn't go to waste while I'm away, Fatcat in a duffel bag on my lap, that Carrick's disbelief, his scorn, is dragging me down.

It's not that I don't still believe in my gift, because I do. But his disbelief makes me wonder if my gift is more sorrow than joy even though I've always believed in its usefulness, ever since the very first time.

I wasn't very old, eighteen maybe. Mom and Aunt Lucy, Gran and I, we'd all been very careful since Mama Amata's visit had saved my life, to avoid photographs of any kind. I'd finished school by correspondence and was working on my welding ticket.

I had to go to school for that, no choice, but I was very careful, quickly getting a reputation for sullenness. That was partly because I was the only girl in a class full of rowdy boys and they scared the hell out of me. But it was partly because I didn't want to trigger my gift.

So I didn't go to the library with them after class, never went to the pub, never asked or answered any questions in class. I passed with flying colors because I worked harder than anyone else. I studied every day until my eyes burned and my head ached. I booked extra time at the welding shop and spend most of my weekends—the time I wasn't studying—in the shop, working with Fred Milton.

And on top of that, I spent hours in the gym, building my upper body strength. Welding isn't a job for the weak.

Fred made it possible for me to be a welder, the first female welder in the state. He showed me how to modify the tools so I could use them with my smaller hands, he gave me routines to work on at the gym, and he believed in me.

I've always been sorry that I didn't spend more time with Fred after I graduated. I think now that he was a lonely man, happy to find someone, anyone really, who loved the work as much as he did.

I didn't know when Fred died. I know I couldn't have saved him, but I could have gone to his funeral.

I found out years after, when I ran into one of my instructors and asked about him.

"Fred?" he said. "Oh, he died about ten years ago. One of the students walked into the shop and there he was, sitting in that big old chair of his as if he'd fallen asleep." He smiled at me. "Which he often did in those days. The doctor said he'd had a massive stroke and died in his sleep, never felt a thing."

I wished then, and still do, that I'd felt it, that I'd known of his death. I wish that I'd carried his picture with me in my wallet and looked at it every single day so that I would know.

But that way lay madness. Because pretty soon I'd be carrying around a trunk full of photographs, waiting to see if someone I knew was going to die. What would I do then?

What I've always done.

Nothing.

I'd graduated and was working as an apprentice in a small shop on the east side of town. I'd found an apartment not far from work and a car that would, reliably, get me from home to work, from work or home to my mother's house, though probably not much further than that.

One Friday night, tired and muscles aching, I

phoned home. "Mom, I'm just too tired to make it tonight. How about we have dinner tomorrow instead?"

"It has to be tonight, Ria. We've got company and it's you they want to see."

The tone of her voice was odd. Not worried, exactly, nor anxious, but slightly off-kilter.

"Company?" Odd enough in itself on a Friday night. Friday nights were family nights. "For me?" Much odder. I didn't really have friends who would drop into my mother's house without warning.

"Ria? I'll see you in half an hour," and she hung up.

Now I was worried. I hurried through the shower and dressing and out to the car. I thanked it for starting without fuss and drove the ten minutes to my mother's house with absolutely no idea of what to expect.

A woman sat on the porch, her hands in her lap, her face puffy from crying and taut with sorrow. I didn't recognize her, not at first.

"Ria?" she said and it was the voice that made me realize who she was, not the face. I recognized her voice because she'd been Juliet in the one and only high school play I'd attended before the accident. I recognized her voice because I'd spent much of the crying time remembering that performance.

"Stephanie? Stephanie Phillips?"

She forced a smile onto her face but it didn't fit and she quickly dropped it. "Yes," she said, "though it's Stephanie Carr now."

"You married Romeo? Jimmy, I mean?"

This time the smile was a little less forced. "I did, right after high school."

I hadn't seen Stephanie Carr for almost four years but her voice was the same and that made me welcome her, welcome the memory of that play and one of the few things that helped me through the crying time.

"What can I do for you, Stephanie?"

Ouch. Wrong question. Maybe she'd just come to visit me but looking at her face, I knew that wasn't true. I knew she needed something and it was something she thought only I could do.

"I remember what happened to you," she said, the answer seemingly unrelated to my question.

"Here," she said, holding out a poster, the kind I'd often have to ignore on the telephone poles on the street. "This is a picture of my Grandpa. He walked away from the seniors' home a couple of days ago and we can't find him."

I didn't know then, and still haven't figured out, how she connected my leaving school with my ability to help her with her grandfather.

"He has Alzheimer's. But we've looked every-where. I just want to find him."

She pushed the paper into my hand. I had care-fully avoided photographs of any kind for almost four years. I had tried, desperately, to ignore my gift.

But here it was seeking me.

If it had been anyone else, I think I could have ignored the plea in her voice. If I hadn't been so tired, I think I might have realized the consequences of picking up that piece of paper and smoothing out the creases before I looked at it.

I put the paper on my knee and closed my eyes. Scared didn't even come close to covering how I felt about looking at this photograph. Terrified, panicked, close to hysterical. And even that wasn't it.

Because I knew, if I looked at this photograph, my life would never be the same again. I would no longer be only *that girl, the welder*. I would no longer be only my mother's daughter and my grandmother's grand-daughter. I'd no longer only be Aunt Lucy's niece.

I would become Ria Sterling, that woman who sees death.

Stephanie watched me, her hands clenched in her lap, her eyes tearing. She watched as I smoothed out the paper, face down on my knee, and watched as I toyed with the edges.

"Please," she said, just one word.

There was no push behind that word, no pressure except in its underlying pain.

I turned over the photograph and bent my head in the near-dark to look at it.

He was going to die. Wherever he was, whatever he was doing, he was going to die. And soon.

I didn't know what to tell her.

"He's going to die, isn't he? Even if we find him, he's going to die."

I didn't raise my head. I couldn't bear to see her face. But I nodded.

A soft hand touched my shoulder, then my chin, forcing my head up.

When my eyes met hers, she said, "Thank you, Ria Sterling. We'll keep looking for him but now we'll look for him differently."

She patted my cold hands with her warm ones.

"Thank you," she said again, and smiled.

Mom, Gran and Aunt Lucy had been watching from the living room window. When they opened the door to the porch, I stood up and went into their waiting embrace.

"You okay?" Gran asked, her sweet lavender powder scent enveloping me.

"I'm okay," I said. "Really."

I guess you never forget your first time. And because Stephanie had smiled at me, I believed that everything was going to be okay.

And basically it has been. Until now.

I hear Mom's footsteps beside the car so I'm expecting her when she opens the trunk and then the backseat to deposit whatever she's packed up for me. Probably way more than I'll need.

Because I've just realized that I won't be at their house for very long. Maybe just until the kitchen window gets fixed and the blinds in the bedroom are replaced.

I put those two things on my mental list of things to do and wait for Mom to start the car.

"Where's my car?" I ask, wondering why I haven't even thought about my baby for days.

"It's in the garage. Carrick drove it home from the job site and put it away for you."

I'm not sure how I feel about Carrick driving my fire-engine red 1967 Mustang convertible, but it isn't good. I don't like the thought of his long legs in my seat and I know I'll have to adjust everything when I get back in the car. That makes me angry.

"Why didn't you get Aunt Lucy to do it?"

"Because," and the reprimand is clear though her voice is low, "we were all busy making sure you were all right. Carrick was the only one who thought about the car.

"And besides, he had to go back to the site anyway. It made sense to give him the keys."

And the keys to the house. But he must have given those back to Mom because he had to break the window to get in last night. All too complicated to consider when I'm riding on a wave of pain.

I must have moaned, because Mom's breathing quickens. All three of them—Mom, Gran and Aunt Lucy—are too attuned to my well-being for comfort.

"I'm okay, Mom. It's just my arms are starting to hurt."

"Do you want to go to emergency?"

"No. I've been in the hospital enough in the past few weeks. No emergency. I want to go home, have a Diet Pepsi, a tuna salad sandwich and some painkillers. They're in my purse." I think about that for a minute. "You did bring my purse, didn't you?"

"I brought everything I could find." She hesitates for a minute and I wonder what it is that she doesn't want to tell me. "You should stay home until the bandages come off," she says. "You can't stay in your place by yourself and Carrick can't be there all the time. He has a job to do."

So do I, though I don't say that out loud. Because

his job is mine, too, right now. We're both committed to finding—God, how did life get so complicated?—Lisa Martin, Frank's killer, the man on the hill behind my house, and whoever it was who blinded me.

Add that to my experiments with my gift, and I'm busy. Too busy to be staying at my mother's for long.

"Did you get the photograph from Carrick?"

"It's in my bag."

I'll wait until I'm alone in my room at home before I touch that photograph.

"Will you put it on my desk? I don't want to touch it by accident."

I feel Mom's worry but also her acquiescence. Whatever happens, she believes in me, and right now I need that belief more than anything else.

I need someone to think I'm doing the right thing. And that someone doesn't seem to be me.

CHAPTER 14

I know the photograph is waiting for me in my room but I postpone it as long as I can. I have breakfast—bacon and eggs and hashbrowns and toast. Gran doesn't cook anymore, but she's damned good at ordering her two daughters around.

And Mom and Aunt Lucy comply. They giggle a bit as they cook, teasing Gran as she orders more and more food.

"Pancakes, now you know how much I love pancakes. With blueberry sauce," Gran says. "Let's have pancakes."

"We're already having bacon and eggs and all the fixings," Aunt Lucy laughs. "We'll have pancakes Sunday like we always do."

"Okay, but fresh squeezed orange juice and black coffee, for sure."

"You'd better be a big tipper," Mom says, "or next time you'll get instant coffee and Tang."

I hear the light smack Gran throws at Mom, the juicer going and the spit-spat of the grease in the frying pan. The coffee smells so good, my mouth starts watering, but I don't drink much coffee. It always smells better than it tastes.

I shift in my chair a little, trying to ignore the pain in my arms, the worry in my head and the photograph in my room. I'm unsuccessful at all three things.

I'm hoping that the painkillers will help settle my arms down to a dull roar but it's taking longer than I expected and I'm getting antsy. I'm not the kind of person who refuses to take cold medicine when I have a cold, or painkillers when I have an injury.

I don't believe in any more pain than is absolutely necessary. Just enough pain to make you stop doing the stupid thing that caused the pain in the first place. Once you've learned your lesson, take the bloody painkillers and get on with your life.

Good philosophy, I think, but not working so well right now. Because this time, even though I'm convinced I've learned whatever lesson I was supposed to learn by pulling the blinds down around me, the painkillers aren't working.

I've lived most of my life without a watch or an alarm clock and have been able to tell within a minute or two what time it is at any time of the day or night. Being unable to guess whether it's day or night, whether it's nine in the morning or three in the afternoon, when added to the blindness, makes my life a series of impossible calculations.

Breakfast time? Lunch? Dinner?

Morning or middle of the night?

Go to bed or get up for a shower?

It's particularly difficult here at home. At least at my house I have things I can do. I can put on a CD, I can play with Fatcat—who is huddled under the bed in my room and probably won't come out until we go home. I can go into the basement and work with weights, although obviously I wouldn't be doing that today.

I can cook my dinner. Okay, I can heat up the soup—I only ever have one kind in the house so I know what to expect—and put butter on the crackers, and then I can do the dishes.

Here, with the triplets hovering over me, all I can do is sit in the dark and think about the photograph on my desk waiting for me, and wonder what in the hell time it is.

Because I'm sure it's way past breakfast time.

I gobble down my bacon, eggs, hashbrowns and toast, drink my freshly squeezed orange juice and pour myself—carefully—my one perfect cup of coffee before I head up the stairs to my room. I don't bump into anything on the way, don't stub my toe on a piece of furniture, don't trip over a mat or a step.

The door to my room no longer squeaks when I open it. When I hit my full-fledged teen rebellion stage, I oiled it so it wouldn't betray me when I snuck out in the middle of the night. I never did sneak out in the middle of the night, but even then, I was thinking ahead, getting prepared for anything, even a complete change in personality.

I smile as the door closes behind me, the hinges smooth and quiet. But the smile only lasts a few short seconds.

The chair is the same one I've been sitting in since I was a teenager, since the desk was added to my room after the crying time. We banged out the wall between my room and the linen closet, adding enough space for a desk, a chair and a couple of bookshelves.

It hasn't changed since those days except that most of the textbooks have gone the way of the dodo. I still keep a computer on the desk, still keep copies of my favorite books on the bookshelves, still—occasionally—come over here to find something that I can't find at my house.

I'm stalling.

And with that thought I sit down, feel around on the desk for the photograph, and pick up the envelope.

Mom has left the photo in the envelope Carrick must have given to her. Considerate, I think, so I wouldn't come upon it by accident.

Carrick must think this is a joke. She can't see, he'll think, so why does she want a photograph? But I couldn't see when I saw Josephine Fairley's death. And now, though I don't have time to think too carefully about it, I'm wondering whether it is sight. Whether I'm right to call what I do *seeing death* instead of sensing it.

I open the flap and gently pull the stiff photographic paper from the envelope. One side is much glossier than the other. I know that's a visual term but it does feel different and it's obvious to me which side of the paper contains the picture of Lisa.

I rub my fingers over the photograph.

I'm not sure how this is going to work. When I was exploring the Yellow Pages, I stopped each time I felt a tingle in my fingertips and that's kind of what I'm expecting this time. If I feel a tingle, I think, that will mean Lisa Martin isn't dead yet.

What I feel isn't anywhere close to a tingle.

It's a full-blown full-out crash of sensation.

It reminds me of what I felt when Frank Morrison

touched me after I'd seen his death in his ID photo, though it's not quite the same.

I clench my teeth together so I won't scream, dropping the photograph to the desktop before I completely lose it and have three almost-hysterical women running up the stairs to save me from myself.

This sensation is different, different than anything I've ever felt before. It's not the tingle I felt in the Yellow Pages, nor the usual *seeing death* sensation, and it's definitely not the Frank Morrison sensation.

It's more like…

I propel the chair away from the desk until it hits the bed and then I pull myself out of the chair and onto the bed. Face down, I try to identify what happened when I touched Lisa Martin's face in the photograph.

If the tingle when I touched the Yellow Pages was the shock you get when you touch the doorknob in the middle of a cold, dry winter, the usual *seeing death* sensation that you feel when you trip over a slightly electrified cattle fence and the Frank Morrison moment a Taser just barely touching my baby toe, this sensation is a jolt in the heart from a Taser.

But I don't know what it means.

Is Lisa dead? Is she dying? Is she lost?

I knew immediately what would happen to her

when my fingers touched the picture of Josephine Fairley. I know intimately what it means when I see a photograph that represents death.

And there was no doubt at all what I felt when I touched Frank Morrison. I didn't just see death, I felt it. I felt it moving from his veins to mine, from his heart to my heart, from his body into mine.

I knew, in that moment with Frank, exactly how it felt to die. He didn't feel it, but I did.

But this isn't what I feel when I force myself back to the desk and the photograph. It's frightening how lost it makes me feel to be so unsure of myself and my gift.

It may be a small gift, but I know it, like I know myself. I know us inside and out. I know how we work.

But now?

I have no fucking idea what this means.

And that means I can't call Carrick Jones and tell him. Because I wouldn't know what to say.

What about, "Carrick? I felt something, something strong when I touched Lisa's photograph."

Or, "I think something's happening with Lisa?"

Maybe even, "I don't know what's going to happen but it'll be…"

It'll be what? Soon? Close? Painful?

I dare myself, then double dare myself, and I

still can't work up the courage to touch the photograph again.

Time passes.

I lie in bed. The photograph sits on the desk. We don't meet.

More time passes.

Finally, when I can't bear the suspense any longer, I place my hand on the glossy side of the photograph. This time, the jolt is just as strong, maybe stronger, but I'm expecting it and I don't drop the photograph.

When I see death in photographs, the sensation fades away if I hold on long enough. It doesn't disappear, it simply fades until it sounds more like Muzak in a first-class office elevator rather than screaming in my ears like a six-piece metal band in a very small venue.

Same with the Yellow Pages. A slight initial tingle, then I'm left with a sensation similar to the way your fingers feel if you've washed dishes in water that's a little too hot. Not a painful burn, but rather the memory of the possibility of pain.

This electric jolt doesn't fade, not even a bit. It stings my hands, then my wrists and forearms, on up into my shoulder joints and across my collarbone.

Then it's in my heart and I feel the pounding, the

quick pulse of blood in every vein, in my ears and throat. I feel it everywhere, in the balls of my feet and the insides of my knees and elbows.

It moves into my lungs. Breathing shallow and fast, I feel myself begin to hyperventilate and I try, I really try, to slow it down.

"Slow," I whisper. "Slow."

But I can't slow them down—not my heart nor my lungs—so I try to pull my hand away from the photograph so I don't faint. But now it won't let me go, won't let me pull away.

The anguish builds, the panting continues, the heart pounds, the lungs begin to spasm.

"Now what?" I gasp out the two words but it's all I can manage. I can't call for Mom or Aunt Lucy, can't even scream, because I can hardly breathe.

And I still can't figure out what it means, what all this means, what I'm supposed to do about it.

I'm dizzy.

I drop my head to the desk and rest my cheek on my hand, which rests on the photograph.

That's all I remember.

CHAPTER 15

"I swear, Ria Sterling, you've fainted more since you've met Carrick Jones than in your entire life."

"Not to mention the amount of time she's spent in the hospital."

"And the time she's spent mooning over his cute butt."

The last voice is Gran's, the other two—interchangeably—are Mom and Aunt Lucy. They stand over me in a semi-circle, their heads nodding in unison, their shadows meeting somewhere over my belly.

"Are you okay now?" Mom asks, but she doesn't sound any too concerned. I think they're all beginning to get used to this newer, frailer version of me.

"I'm fine," I reply, trying without success to pull myself up off the floor.

"Sure you are." Aunt Lucy kneels down behind me and helps me to sit up. "You look great, if you like the pale as milk with a slight tinge of green look."

Mom bends down beside Aunt Lucy and helps me to my feet, then over to lie on the bed. None of them asks me what I'm doing on the floor looking like Ophelia in the stream, none of them frets over me.

I'm sure underneath their determinedly cheerful voices they're worried, but they're trying not to show it and I'm grateful.

"Thanks, you guys. I'm fine, really."

Gran hands me half a glass of water. I imagine the glass was full when she started and I expect that the stairs are a bit damp but I appreciate the thought.

I drink the water and try to decide how much I'm going to tell them. The trouble is that I don't really know anything and if I tell them that, they'll just worry.

But I need some help and I'm not going to get it from Jones. I'll call him once I've hashed this out with my family, tell them what we sort of know, and then leave it at that.

"I'd love a cup of tea," I say and listen as the three of them scramble down the stairs to make me one. I follow more slowly and soon—as we've done thousands of times over the years—the three of us are sitting at the kitchen table, the kettle gently steaming on the stove and the smell of Bengal Spice tea perfuming the air.

"How long has Uncle Jim been keeping track of all the people who come to see me?"

I don't ask how he knows who they are, sometimes I only know their names and nothing else. I don't charge money but I do try and obtain a little information from them. Their names, their home towns. More as a way to make them comfortable than anything else. I keep all that information on index cards in a recipe file box in my office.

I've been wondering how he knew who they were since he showed up with the letters at the interrogation but I've been distracted and the question kept getting pushed to the bottom of the list.

Gran hums and haws. "What do you mean keeping track? He isn't keeping track, not really. He just worries about you. Not like us," she says. "We know what you're capable of."

She's lying.

I wonder why Mom and Aunt Lucy aren't coming to the aid of Gran but I don't let it stop me.

"I think I need to talk to him," I say, "because I don't want anyone…"

I don't want anyone what? Knowing who comes to see me? Knowing what I've told them? Knowing how often I feel like a failure?

Because I'm willing to bet that out of the hundreds of people who have come to see me over the years, I've only been able to tell less than a quarter of them what they've come to hear.

Your father/mother/brother/lover/sister/child/grandparent is going to die.

"I'm grateful to Uncle Jim," I say. "He really helped me at the police station. But I need to know how he got those names." I hesitate and then say, "Pass me the phone, okay?"

I hear the three of them scuffling their feet under the table and a few throat clearings before Aunt Lucy, obviously designated spokesperson for this difficult task, speaks.

"We gave him the file box."

"What?" I squeak, my voice failing me along with the rest of my body.

"We gave him the file box," my mother repeats. "We've been worried for a long time that something like this might happen and we wanted to make sure we had some defence to any charge they might have against you."

Gran pats me on the shoulder, her lavender scent softening my anger. "We did it because we love you, girl, you know that."

Mom continues, "And we give him the new names every month so he can keep up to date."

"He has a computer listing at his office of everyone that's come to see you," Aunt Lucy says. "What if something happened to you? Those names might be the only way to find you."

I think about the hours Uncle Jim must have spent to get those letters and how worried he must have been to allow the family to intrude on my—and my clients'—privacy this way.

"I understand," I say, "but ask me the next time, okay?"

Because I do see the worth of this list, in fact, I'm pretty sure, now that I think about it, that the man who's been watching me, the man who blinded me, is on that list.

"Right now, though, I need to figure out what happened to me when I touched Lisa's picture. I need to know what it meant and I need—" I shudder at the thought of doing it, but there's no choice "—to do it again.

"I'll deal with Uncle Jim and the list later. But, Gran," I ask as I drag myself out of the chair and start heading toward the stairs, "will you call Uncle Jim and ask him to send over the list he has? I want to compare it with my list and see if anyone jumps out at me. His list will be easier to read than mine."

That was an understatement. The cards I use to record my information on are a mess. They are covered in tear and food stains, some of them ripped, on many of them the ink has faded until it is barely legible.

But those file cards, like the old card catalogues in the libraries, are full of information. Some of them have notations of who the person was looking for, information about when they'd last been seen and where.

I wrote down anything I remembered that seemed important at the time and a whole bunch of stuff that wasn't, or didn't appear to be, but that I thought was interesting. So those cards—unlike, I'd be willing to bet, Uncle Jim's list—recorded more than just facts, they included my impressions of people, of their quest, of their families and their lives.

In some cases, I knew more about those people than their families did. In many cases, I knew more about them than a therapist would.

Because by the time they got to me, they were at the end of the line. They were desperate, willing to try anything, and they'd talked to everyone they could think of about their problem and gotten no results.

Mostly, I just listened, and mostly that's all they wanted. Someone to listen to their stories about their loved one, someone who believed them when they said, "I don't think she's dead. I'd know if she was dead. I would."

Enough, I think, the cards are for later. Right now, it's all about Lisa. And pain.

I try to ignore the memory of the pain I experienced touching her photograph and the pain I'm feeling in my arms just walking up the stairs to my room.

It's not possible, of course. You can't ignore pain, not really, but if you're lucky, you can push it to the back of your mind. And that's what I'm trying to do, trying to overlay the aches from the fall and the sharp zing of the cuts in my arms with the urgency of my task.

It's not working.

But I do manage to restrain any groans from escaping as I slide up the stairs. Two out of the three of them are following me.

Aunt Lucy and Mom, I expect. Gran will be on the phone to Uncle Jim reporting in on my request and reassuring him that he's done the right thing.

I wouldn't be surprised if Gran disappears for several hours so she and Uncle Jim can spend a relaxing day—though how you can call it relaxing is beyond me—at the casino. The two of them play roulette for hours on end and they never, ever come home with less money than they went with. Though,

I have to admit, they also seldom come home with any winnings, either.

I sit down in the chair at the desk, Mom and Aunt Lucy hover behind me. All three of us look at the photograph. Okay, I don't exactly look, but it's the same thing. Their hands settle on my shoulders and I take a deep breath.

At least this time I know what to expect.

Knowing what's going to happen doesn't help at all. I'm dragged into the electrical whirlpool yet again but this time—because of Mom and Aunt Lucy—I'm able to get past the shock and settle into the *seeing*.

Lisa Martin is still alive. But not for long. And for the first time ever, I sense something that will help the police find her in time. I don't exactly see where she is, no street numbers, no landmarks, but, because I've been to the neighborhood, I recognize the location. She's on the east side, and I can pinpoint it within a few blocks.

I don't even question my certainty.

"Call Carrick and tell him that I know where Lisa Martin is. And she's still alive, though—" my voice drops to a whisper "—not for long."

CHAPTER 16

The rush of police officers I've been expecting doesn't arrive. In fact, it takes almost three hours for Carrick Jones, alone and as angry as a hornet, to show up on my doorstep.

Obviously, my vision is not a priority.

Aunt Lucy has driven me home and has parked across the street, promising to leave the minute Carrick shows up. She and I have been talking on our respective cell phones for much of the three hours, but not about anything important. I think she's just trying to keep me calm.

Because as the time progresses, I get angrier and angrier.

"Where in the hell is he?"

Aunt Lucy is calm. "He's probably busy, Ria. Don't forget he's a police officer, he has other cases than this one."

"I don't care."

I'm sounding like a twelve-year-old but I don't care about that, either. I've just had a revelation, one that might save a life and I want to do just that. It may be the only life I ever save, but I want that one.

"I want to save her life," I say to Lucy, "how hard is that to understand?"

"Not hard at all. But don't forget Carrick's only known you for a very little while and you did kind of get off on the wrong foot."

"Yeah, if you can call predicting his partner's death and being blamed for it the wrong foot. I'd call it a disaster of epic proportions."

Lucy and I both laugh and settle into gossip about Gran and Uncle Jim. This, as always, manages to keep me entertained and relatively cheerful for a time but the conversation inevitably swings back to Carrick.

"Do you think I'm using my gift because I'm obsessed with Jones?" I haven't spoken this thought out loud before, not even to myself, but I want to know what Aunt Lucy thinks.

"Do you think that?"

"I don't know. I'm attracted to him. I believe we're meant to be together. But I also think Lisa Martin can be saved if he listens to me. And there's something else, too."

Lucy hums into the receiver. She often does this when she's thinking and I find it relaxing. It means she's really thinking about what I've said and what she knows about the situation. She's not going to give me a pat answer.

"I think," she pauses, humming again, "I think that you'd never use your gift for the wrong reasons. I think that the two things—saving Lisa Martin and your feelings for Carrick—have gotten so tangled up you can't tell the difference. But I can.

"Yes, you want to see Carrick. You love him."

I gulp and nod my head, knowing she can't see me and knowing that she doesn't need to.

"But you also want to save Lisa. And I think that saving her will be good for both of you. You both want the same thing—you want to save someone."

I nod again.

"He's coming. Call us when you know anything," and Aunt Lucy hangs up.

Her car hums like she does—it's a hybrid—as it drives away and Carrick's police-issue monster roars into the driveway a few moments later. Even the car sounds angry and I wonder if I should call Aunt Lucy to come back.

This conversation needs to be held in private.

The car door slams, the boot heels pound on the

steps, the door bell chimes, but even its usual sweet-sounding bells sound pissed off. I try yelling over them to "come in," but he doesn't hear me because the door starts shaking with the force of his fist against the oak.

"Wait just a minute, okay?" I yell, feeling my way to the door. "I'm blind, remember? I can't get to the door that fast."

I'd been meaning to leave it unlocked but Aunt Lucy wouldn't let me.

The first lock is a simple one. I turn the handle and pull the door, trying to ignore the pounding and the deep voice yelling, "Open the damn door, Ria, or I'm going to break it down."

"I'm trying, I'm trying," I yell back, but Aunt Lucy is nothing if not thorough and she's locked the deadbolt as well, and it's taking me a few minutes to find it.

In the meantime, Jones is getting angrier and angrier, and he's losing whatever miniscule dab of patience he arrived with. "Open. The. Damn. Door."

He hammers against it again. "Now."

He falls across the doorsill as I yank it open. "There. You happy now?" I say, standing—at least I think I am—over his sprawled body.

"Yeah, I'm happy," he says, standing up, his voice

now coming from above instead of below me. "Happy as a damn clam."

"Good. Though why people say clams are happy is beyond me. Would you be happy, stuck in damp sand all day just waiting for someone to come along and pluck you up and cook you? No way. I think it's a lousy metaphor."

"What do you want?" Carrick Jones leads me down the hall to the kitchen, his hand adding another set of bruises to my already sore arms.

I'm wearing long sleeves so he hasn't noticed the bandages—obviously didn't notice them when he came to look for the man on the hill either—but he drops his hand and I suspect he's seen the winces I'm trying to conceal.

"What's wrong with your arms?"

He wrenches the sleeves up over the bandages. "Now what? I don't know how you've survived all these years. You're more trouble than anyone I've ever met."

"I wasn't any trouble at all until I met you, you know. I was living a perfectly normal, perfectly reasonable life until you showed up on my doorstep. This," I point at the bandages over my eyes, the bandages on my arms, the burgeoning bruises he's just given me, the windows in the kitchen, and give a rather vague wave toward my bedroom blinds, "is all your fault."

Carrick gives a quiet harumph and takes my hand, gently this time, leading me into the kitchen. He pushes me down into the chair that faces the window, the sun streaming in and warming me from the outside in. He's rattling around in the cupboards and the fridge.

"Coffee okay?"

I nod. My eyes are closed, have been beneath the bandages for days. I've forgotten what it's like to have them open, but I pretend to close them anyway and lift my face to the sun. *No more than a few days,* I think, *and I'll be able to see again.* I avoid thinking about the nightmares I've been having about being blind forever. I just enjoy the sun and the sound of Carrick puttering in my kitchen.

The floorboards squeak and a shadow cools one side of my face as he sits down in the chair opposite me. "Here," he says, wrapping my hand around a mug. "It's hot. Be careful."

"Thanks, I've been dreaming about coffee a lot lately. It's the one thing I can't make like this. Blind, I mean. Hot chocolate, no problem. I just use the packages. Same with tea. But coffee's different. It's too complicated when I can't see."

The first sip is perfect, just the right amount of cream, and the coffee's rich and dark and smooth, just like Carrick. Although I have this feeling that the smoothness is wearing thin around the edges.

It's been replaced with anger.

At me.

"I'm not angry with you," he says, as if he's reading my mind. "It's the situation. It's Frank and Lisa Martin and the man on the hill. If there was a man on the hill," he adds under his breath.

He's forgotten that my hearing has become hyper-acute since I've been wearing these bandages. Or maybe I never told him. We haven't had too many normal conversations since we've met.

And we won't be having one today, either.

"Carrick, I think I have an idea where Lisa Martin might be."

He looks at me, I know he does. His right eyebrow is tilted ever so slightly upward on the outside edge, the line between his brows gets even deeper, his eyes glaze over and his nostrils flare. He rolls his shoulders before he says one single, ultra sarcastic word. "Please."

"I'm not kidding."

"You know what's the worst part? I know you're not kidding. I wish you were. It would make things all so much easier."

Maybe for you, I think. But not for me.

"You want me to be kidding because you don't

believe in my gift. I don't understand how you can't. You've seen proof."

I fight back the tears and concentrate on the anger. If I start crying now, I'm toast. Being angry is much more sensible.

"You don't believe me because you have some… Some something," I say, feeling stupid, but also knowing that I'm right. There is some something going on with Jones and it's not about me.

"Some *something?*"

Once again the sarcasm, once again I picture *that* face, the one that pisses me off more than anything else.

My chair crashes as I push away from the table, reaching for his face. I don't know whether it's because he doesn't expect it or because he's trying to be careful around the crazy blind lady, but I get my hands on his face and I hold on. Tight. He might have a few bruises to match mine.

I lean in as close as I can get, until I feel his breath on my face, and the warmth of his skin. And then I lean in a little closer.

"Now. You. Listen."

Jones is anything but stupid. Aggravating, yes. Stubborn, even more so. Angry, oh you bet. But he's not stupid. He shrugs and settles back into his chair.

I settle in between his thighs, my lips at his right ear, my hands tight on his face, and I tell him.

I tell him everything that's happened since yesterday morning. I tell him about feeling the man on the hillside. I tell him about the blinds and the cuts and bruises. He takes a quick breath and I feel his palms running, slowly, softly, over my arms for a moment before he settles back again.

I tell him about the photograph. I tell him that it felt like a Taser jolt.

"And have you felt a Taser jolt? Not—" I feel him hold up his hands to stop me from squeezing his face any tighter "—that I think you might have, of course. I'm just asking."

"No," I say, "I haven't been stopped by a Taser. But I have worked on construction sites for a very long time and once, when I was very young and very stupid, I did hit a live wire, so I can guess what it feels like."

"How long did you spend in hospital that time?"

"Not long. Only a couple of days while they made sure there were no residual effects."

"Were there?" He sounds like he's hoping that the electrocution is the reason I am who I am, as if that would be a perfectly reasonable explanation for the way I am, for the gift.

"No," and I answer the question he's carefully not asking. "I've had this gift since I was very young."

"Oh," and he waits for the rest of the story.

So I tell him I know that Lisa Martin is still alive. I tell him we can save her. I tell him she's somewhere in the vicinity of Oak Heights because I can see the houses and the only place those little one story mini-ranchers have been built is that single subdivision.

"There can't be more than a hundred houses there," I say, though now I'm talking about her I'm pretty sure she's not in a house. "But I don't think she's in a house. I think she's in the woods somewhere."

"Those woods are just barely big enough to get lost in. Why hasn't she found her way out?"

"I don't know. But I do know if we don't find her soon she won't find her way out at all."

Carrick is weighing my story. I feel him still for a moment, as if he's stopped moving, maybe even stopped breathing. I know this is a big decision for him so I, too, slow everything down. And I don't move.

And I don't move until my arms and fingers hurt from holding on without either tightening or loosening my grip. I don't move until I wonder if we're locked in some kind of weird vacuum of time and space. I don't move until he shifts a little in his chair and says, "Okay."

"Okay?"

"Is there anyone else with her?"

"I don't know. I've told you everything. She's not in a house, she's in the woods, she's somewhere near Oak Heights. And you have to find her. You have to find her *now* or she won't make it."

When I step away from Carrick, I stumble a little. His arms reach and steady me before I can fall, and then they stay where they are, wrapped around my waist. I drop my arms from his face to his neck and hold on, tight, because suddenly I can't bear to move away from his warmth.

"Thanks, Ria," he says. I'm not sure he means it but I'll take it as an apology anyway.

"I have to go." He stands up, kisses me on the cheek—I'm astonished—and then hands me the phone from the counter. "Call your Aunt Lucy. She's probably somewhere around the block waiting to see what happens."

I laugh and call her. She is only a block away, shopping, she says, but Carrick and I and Aunt Lucy all know better.

While we're waiting, he calls the station and they set in motion the search and rescue teams, the K-9 teams, the urban search teams, the police search teams. He talks so fast I can barely keep up but I can picture the activity as the entire system swings into place to find Lisa Martin.

I hope they find her. I hope she's going to be okay. She's been missing so long, though, I worry that even if they find her in time, she'll be irreparably damaged. And I hope, when they do find her, that she believes being alive is worth all the pain she's suffered and all the pain she's going to suffer in the hospital and in rehab.

How do I know that? I don't. I'm just guessing. If she's missing in those woods and has been since she went missing, it's because she's trapped somewhere or she's lying injured somewhere and that can't mean anything good.

"I'll call you when I hear anything," Carrick says. "I'll call you at your mother's, right?"

There's nothing like a question in that statement, it's an order couched in question form.

"Right," I say. "Aunt Lucy's here now and I'll go back to Mom's."

He's already forgotten me, I think, as he hurries out the door with a "take her home" to Aunt Lucy as he passes her on the porch.

"Does he believe you?" she asks.

"I'm not sure, but he's acting as if he does. It doesn't matter, not really, because he's trying to find her and that's all that counts."

Aunt Lucy ruffles my hair and says, "You're right, Ria. Finding Lisa is all that matters."

CHAPTER 17

My mother's house isn't that close to Oak Heights but even a few miles away we hear the helicopters over the woods. The TV is tuned to the local news station and they're keeping us up to date about the search.

"The police have had a tip that Lisa Martin—missing since the morning of the fifteenth—is somewhere in the Oak Heights area. They're combing the woods."

While the announcer continues speaking, Mom whispers that they pan back to show the search teams heading into the woods, "and have set up a mobile headquarters on Miller Street."

All of us, including Gran and Uncle Jim who have hurried back from the casino after hearing the news, sit in the living room and wait.

We've seen Lisa's photograph, know about her husband and children and job. In some ways, in many ways, I know Lisa Martin better than I know my coworkers. And that's not a good thing.

To distract myself from the ongoing coverage, to help me ignore the constant anxiety the waiting causes, I turn to Uncle Jim. "I need a list of everybody who's been working on that Marathon worksite. More than a list."

He pats my hand. "Already compiling. I have the list but I'm working on more information. You know, criminal records, stuff like that."

I laugh, because if I don't, I'll cry. It's a terrible state of affairs, as Uncle Jim would no doubt put it, that I have to check on my fellow workers this way.

But now that I know—and I do know, though Carrick doesn't believe me—that Lisa Martin wasn't kidnapped, I need to find out who's watching me, who would want me blinded. Because it's not about Lisa Martin.

It's about me.

I'm not so sure about Frank Morrison's death.

"Uncle Jim? Do the police know anything more about Detective Morrison's murder?"

I hear him taking a sip from the glass of scotch Mom brought him when he and Gran arrived back from the casino. No one in this family drinks it, we drink red wine and beer, but we splurge on the expensive stuff for Uncle Jim.

"Not much, Ria. The autopsy's done, they know how he died, and when."

I try not to think of the images this statement conjures in my mind. I got enough of an idea about the size of that machete when the police were questioning me about the murder.

"That's it?"

"That's all I've heard."

"That's unusual, isn't it? I mean, for them not to know anything about his murder? He's a cop and they throw everything they've got into finding a cop killer, right?"

"Yes, Ria, they do. They have a task force, they have daily briefings, they've got dozens of officers out on the streets trying to find witnesses, they're combing Frank's files. But so far, nothing."

I don't even question Uncle Jim's knowledge. He's been in this town for so long, knows so many people, has so many connections and strings to pull, that he probably knows as much as George York, the chief.

He certainly knows more than Carrick. But that more basically still amounts to nothing.

"Why do you want a list of the people you were

working with?" Uncle Jim asks, taking another sip of his scotch. The light tinkle of the ice cubes makes me thirsty and I head for the kitchen for a beer, Jim following me.

"Why did you start one?" I counter.

The kitchen is warm with the light of the late sun and fragrant with the odors of Mom's cooking. The three women—as always—are laughing as they cook a pork roast, green beans and scalloped potatoes. I know they're doing it for me because it's my favorite meal. I'd rather have scalloped potatoes than almost anything else, especially my mom's homemade scalloped potatoes with plenty of cheese.

Instead of returning to the living room and the buzz of the TV news anchor, I sit down at the table and let the normal homey sounds and smells of this place relax me.

I was hoping to have this conversation out of earshot of my family, but I think now that it doesn't matter. They'll find out anyway. Uncle Jim will tell Gran, who will tell Mom and Aunt Lucy. They'll pretend they don't know, I'll pretend I don't know they know, and what's the point?

"I think," I take a drink and wait for the other three to sit down around me, "that what's been happening—the welding flash, the man on the hill, aren't about Frank Morrison or Lisa Martin. I think they're about me."

Uncle Jim gives a grunt of assent. The three women are silent.

"I also think…" I'm not sure I can say the next part out loud until Mom puts her hand over mine. "I also think that Frank Morrison's death might be about me as well. I think Carrick was right when he blamed me for it."

"What makes you think that?" Uncle Jim, as always, asks the right question.

Because this isn't about what's happened to me. I'm going to be fine, maybe even soon. But Frank Morrison is going to be dead forever.

"Just a feeling," I reply. "Too many coincidences."

"The biggest coincidence…" Aunt Lucy hesitates and I wonder if she'll say what she's thinking. "The oddest thing is that Ria hasn't had a single person come looking for her since this all started."

I've been too discombobulated—one of Gran's favorite words and one that perfectly expresses my mental state at this moment—to even notice that I've not had a single person show up at my doorstep with a photograph. It's not completely unheard of for me to go two weeks without *someone* showing up, but it is unusual.

"I hadn't thought of that," Mom says, "but you're right. And it can't be because she hasn't been at home. They all seem to know—and how do they know anyway?—that if she's not at her place, she'll be at ours."

"It has happened before. Two or three weeks without a single person showing up," I say, trying to stop them from making a big deal of it and knowing, absolutely, that it won't work.

"But not for years," Gran says. "Not since—" I can almost hear the wheels turning in her head "—five years ago last summer. More people know about you now. And every year you get more people. Five years since it happened last time."

Okay, so it is a big deal, part and parcel of the whole thing that's weirding me out.

It's obvious that I've been silent too long because I hear them shuffling restlessly in their chairs. But I don't know how to answer them.

Instead I change the subject.

"How long until the roast is ready?" I ask. "I need to go for a walk if we have time. Who's up for it?"

Uncle Jim and Gran decline, but Mom and Aunt Lucy are ready to go. We have an hour, the weather's good, and the TV's not coming with us. Plus Mom and Aunt Lucy feel safe leaving because the dinner's basically ready and Uncle Jim will make sure that Gran doesn't touch anything.

I haven't been outside except to go from some building to the car for so long it feels as if I've been let out of school for the summer. It's cool but the air is fresh and clean on my face, the birds are singing and I feel better than I have in weeks.

Living in the dark hasn't been easy but it's not until now, when I'm outside, the sun on my skin, the air on my face, that I realize just how hard it has been, how much I've missed mowing the lawn, walking in the woods back of my house, working.

God, I've missed working. It's normal, being on a worksite, wielding the welding torch, making something right, putting things together and knowing that they're going to hold.

Working is the thing that's kept me sane all these years.

We walk the way we've walked ever since I can remember. Down the block, around the corner and into the park. The kids are laughing and screaming in the playground, the wind is rustling the leaves on the trees, the gardener is mowing the grass on the soccer field.

Mom and Aunt Lucy hold my arms, one on each side of me. They quietly murmur, "step up," or "we're crossing the road now," when necessary but don't say much of anything else.

The three of us sit on *our* bench, the one with its back to the tiny patch of birch and pine trees—an odd combination, I know, but I don't think the parks board understood that the two types of trees don't go together and they seem to be doing fine.

That tiny piece of land scared me as a child but I grew out of it, using it as a place to hide and play as a teenager. We all did, everyone who lived in the neighborhood.

But today someone is in there. Someone is watching me. I feel it. Again.

"It's him," I whisper to my mom and Aunt Lucy. "He's behind us and he's watching me. Don't turn around," I say urgently, "I don't want him to suspect that I know he's there."

I turn slightly to get closer to Mom. "Did you bring your cell phone?"

"No. Lucy? Did you?"

"What do we do? I can turn around," Lucy says after searching her pockets and finding no cell phone, but stops as I grab her arm.

"Don't turn around, don't let him know we know he's there. I want to see if he'll get closer."

"Close enough to see who it is?" Mom asks, her voice strong and as solid as she is.

"Absolutely," Aunt Lucy replies. "He's done enough damage already."

We wait, and it seems as if that's what I've been doing for days. I don't think I've waited so much in my whole life.

But I'll sit on this bench for as long as it takes.

"Lucy," Mom says, her voice sounding almost normal, "what's up at work? Are Tom and Cheryl still seeing each other?"

"Thanks, Mom," I whisper, and then chime in with her efforts to get the conversation going and fool whoever's watching me into thinking we don't know he's there. "I saw Cheryl a couple of weeks ago with another guy."

"You did?" Lucy asks. "*I* saw Tom buying an engagement ring the other day."

"That doesn't sound good," Mom says, and I nod in agreement.

We talk about Tom and Cheryl—who I've never met and probably never will—for another few minutes but I'm only half paying attention. I'm trying to somehow pinpoint the feeling, the one that tells me I'm being watched, but the harder I try, the more amorphous the feeling becomes, until I can't tell whether there's anyone there or not.

"Mom? Aunt Lucy? I think he's gone. Take a look, will you?"

Five minutes later, we're heading back to the house, arguing about whether or not I should call Carrick. In the end, I win the battle, but only because of Lisa Martin.

"I don't want to distract him. Lisa needs him way more than I do right now."

And both of them understand that. We're a family who understands and lives with other people's needs. And we've learned to live with the danger the gift puts me in. Physically. Emotionally. With the law.

I grin at that thought.

"He's the biggest danger I've ever been in," I say. Mom says, "You're not kidding," and I realize I've said it out loud.

Aunt Lucy laughs. "Men are always the biggest danger to a woman. And women are always men's biggest danger. It's just the way the world works." She laughs again. "Look at poor Tom and Cheryl."

She doesn't say anything about my father or about the man she once loved and lost. She doesn't say anything about Carrick Jones. But I know she's worried about me.

Well, those risks are going to be a lot less to-morrow. Because tomorrow I'm going to the doctor and getting the damn bandages removed.

CHAPTER 18

We have to take Uncle Jim's car to the doctor's office—it's the only one big enough—because everyone insists on coming with me while I have the bandages removed.

They also all insist on being in the room with me while it happens.

The doctor isn't happy about it, but Uncle Jim is persuasive and the women are unmoveable. The room feels a little too hot and way too crowded but I know if the doctor hasn't managed to get them to wait outside, there's no way I'm going to accomplish anything.

The doctor explains what he's doing. "I'm turning the lights out now." His voice hardens. "None of you move, not a bit. And don't talk either."

I smell the light aftershave he wears—it's tangy, maybe a little citrusy—as he leans over me. I imagine him wearing one of those metal thingamabobbys around his forehead with a light at the front. I imagine the light on my face.

His hands touch the bandages at the side of my head and I hear and feel the scissors snipping away at the bandages.

"Ria, I'm taking the bandages off now. Don't try to open your eyes yet. I need to flush them before you do that."

As the bandages unwind from my head, I immediately feel lighter. I know they can't have weighed more than a few ounces, but the removal of them changes everything.

"Don't move," he says, sharply, and I realize I've been turning my head this way and that to take advantage of the lovely feeling of weightlessness.

"Sorry," I say and sit as still as I can.

When the final turn of the bandages is done, he says again, "Sit still, very still." I feel him lift the smaller bandages from my eyes and now they're only eyes, not eyes covered with something. I could open them, I think, but I don't.

I'm scared.

"Don't worry," the doctor says, "and don't move," as if he's reading my mind, but I know he's not. He doesn't have to. He must do this all the time, not just with welders, but with people who have operations on their eyes, or damage done to them.

"I'm going to flush your eyes now. It'll be cool on your eyes, and maybe sting a little, but don't move, okay? It won't take too long."

He hands me a small towel. "Don't touch your eyes with it. Just keep it under your chin to catch the drops."

I hold the towel to my chin and try not to flinch as he tilts my head back. I suspect I'm not very successful as he says, "Ria, it's going to be okay. Just don't move, all right?"

I have the dark glasses the nurse told me to bring with me in one hand, the towel in the other. The solution is cool on my face and it tickles as it drips down my neck. A shower would be better than this fine, light trickle—it makes me shiver.

The doctor gently pats the moisture from my eyes. It doesn't hurt. "Okay," he says. "Ria, hand me the glasses. I'm going to put them on and then when I tell you, I want you to open your eyes. Remember that they'll probably sting a little and if it hurts too much, close them again."

I swear to myself that no matter how much they hurt, I'm going to keep my eyes open. Ten days is too long to be without sight—I'm not going to let it go on any longer.

"Now," he says, his hand on my shoulder. "Remember that it's dark in this room so you won't see much of anything. I've got my hand in front of your face and you should be able to see that.

"Open your eyes."

It isn't as easy as I expect it to be. In all the dreams I've been having about this moment, I open my eyes and there it is—the world—at least the small part of it contained in this room. The doctor's office, the doctor, the eye chart on which I can read every single line. And of course, I see Carrick.

But today this isn't what happens. I open my eyes under the sunglasses and I see...

Light. I see light. And that's a good sign because if the blindness had been permanent I wouldn't see anything. But the light hurts and I close my eyes again.

"Open your eyes, Ria. I know they hurt but I need to examine them."

I open my eyes again. This time I see light plus a blur of movement as the doctor's face and hands come closer to me.

The family is murmuring in the background. They sound enthusiastic, but whenever do they not?

"I'm going to take off the glasses, okay? Close your eyes until I tell you to open them."

His cool hands lift the glasses from my face.

"Now."

I open my eyes yet again. I'm beginning to feel like one of those dolls whose eyes stay closed when they're lying flat and blink open when you stand or sit them up.

The sharp stab of light makes my eyes water and, for the first time in what feels like forever, I actually feel the tears run down my face. I want to cheer.

A fine thin stream of light runs across my eyes. "Follow the light, Ria," the doctor says and I can almost see his face. At least now I know it's a face and not a blur anymore.

"You look fine. You're going to have some pain for a couple of days and you should wear the glasses even in the house. I've written you a prescription for some painkillers but if you're not feeling better by Tuesday, come back and see me. Otherwise, you're good to go back to work in a week."

I hear the collective sigh of relief from the peanut gallery and I grin over at them.

"Hi, guys," I say. "Nice to see you."

And I mean it. It's great to see them. They're still a little blurry and I can tell I'm not going to be driving or doing any TV watching—for today at least—but it feels great to be walking on my own without someone holding onto my arm.

I feel safer, too. I hadn't realized how unsafe I did feel without sight—too much going on to worry too much about that—until now, when I feel better.

I've always loved the darkness, embraced it, really. But that was when I could see something, even just the outlines of furniture or the windows against the dark walls. When the darkness was absolute, it scared me.

I walk out of the room determined to get back my comfortable relationship with the night.

The nurse in the waiting room is listening to the radio, as are the few patients sitting in the orange fibre chairs.

"What's up?" Gran asks, never one to ignore the potential for interesting gossip.

"They've found that woman who's been missing."

Gran looks over at me. I can see that she doesn't want to ask the next question in my presence in case the answer is the wrong one, but at a nod from me, she does. "Is she alive?"

"They say she is, but she's been trapped in her car the whole time so they don't know how she's going to be."

I slump against the nearest body, which happens to be Aunt Lucy. "It's okay, Ria," she says. "Let's go home, okay?"

We turn on the radio in the car but we've already heard all the information there is. They don't know anything else, though they're happy to speculate.

"I'll call Carrick when we get to the house." Uncle Jim is the best person for this task. Carrick's angry at me, Mom or Aunt Lucy probably wouldn't get through, and Gran isn't even in the running.

"Thanks." I don't expect he'll know much more, but he might be able to tell us how she got there and why no one had found her until now.

I wonder if it's just me who thinks that people getting trapped in their cars is becoming a common occurrence, but Mom's words stop me wondering.

"This is the third person in the past couple of years who this has happened to. There was that kid up north—he was in his car for over two weeks. And that young woman somewhere in Washington State. Now Lisa Martin."

"I never heard of it before this," Aunt Lucy says, "but you're right. I wonder why."

"Maybe they just never found them until they were already…"

Uncle Jim has the sense to stop the sentence before he says the word. But I hear it anyway. Dead.

The ride home is a joy—and not just because they've found Lisa Martin alive. I'm not quite ready to celebrate that event. There's no guarantee she's going to stay that way.

And when I think about that, I know I'm going to spend the next few days with her picture, though I'm not sure how my gift will react to it now.

Not once has someone called me to say that they saved their brother or sister or father or lover. No one has ever called me to say that they found their father just in time to tell him how much they loved him.

I will touch Lisa Martin's photo when I get home but for now I shake these thoughts from my head and settle down to enjoy the ride. I *will* enjoy the things that I can see.

It's cloudy, which is a good thing given the condition of my eyes, but I can see the shape of things. Trees and buildings and cars. And they're all limned with a faint glow of red, as if the sun, though hidden, is still conscious of their presence and wants to be sure that they're conscious of the sun.

It's beautiful.

CHAPTER 19

Uncle Jim doesn't manage to speak to Carrick Jones, but he does speak to George York, the chief. Lisa Martin's car plunged off the road in a short-lived but violent storm. I remember that morning, the way the clouds raced in, turning the streets slick with oil and foot-deep puddles, then disappeared as quickly as they had appeared. She and her car ended up one hundred feet down the embankment almost buried in leaves and overhung by trees. No one knew she'd be on that road, no one could have seen the car until the wind of the last few days blew some of the leaves away.

So, thanks, Ria Sterling. That's it. We don't need you anymore. He didn't say that, not exactly, but I can tell that's what he means.

Except they do need me. Especially Carrick.

But it's not going to be easy to convince him of that.

"Mom. Aunt Lucy. Jim. We need to continue going over the names of the men who work with me. I want to eliminate as many of them as we can."

"And how are we going to do that?" Mom's concern is clear. "We don't know what we're looking for."

"I've already eliminated a lot of them. There's only the men who started work for Marathon after Ria, or at the same time. Anyway, when the new job started. So if we're assuming that it's someone who's looking specifically for her, it will be someone who followed her to the job site."

I smile at Uncle Jim and can almost see the expression on his face. "I think you're right. We need to make some assumptions or we'll never get anywhere. We might as well use that one."

"What other ways can we eliminate some of them?" Aunt Lucy is making sandwiches and Gran is stirring the soup. It's on the lowest heat setting because she never manages to pay attention for very long. Gran ruined two whole sets of pots before Mom and Aunt Lucy figured out how to stop her.

"We can't question them, that's what we need Carrick for," I say, knowing everyone else is thinking the same thing. "And we can't follow them. But we know…"

Uncle Jim is the one who says it, articulating the words I am avoiding.

"I think this has to be about Ria's gift. There's no other reason anyone would be after her."

"Not my charm and personality and good looks? You mean I don't have a stalker?"

They all laugh, as I had meant them to. We're scared enough and making light of this doesn't cost me anything.

Mom reaches across the table and touches my hand. "How are we going to find out if anyone who came to see you is also working for Marathon?"

"We're going to cross reference the list of names from Marathon with my cards."

I say this but I know it's not going to be easy and it won't be completely accurate, either. I've had people come to see me whose names won't be on the cards for a whole bunch of reasons.

They didn't want to give me their name.

I was too busy and didn't write them down and then forgot.

They lied to me.

Uncle Jim is delegated to return to his office and get the list of Marathon names and Mom is delegated to drive me home to pick up my index card box of names. I also want—though Mom doesn't know this—to touch Lisa Martin's photograph.

I concentrate on the view out the window, watching the sun cast shadows on the sidewalks, enjoying the colors of the cars speeding past, even smiling when I can discern the green-yellow-red sequence of the stoplights.

The trip to my house is only a few minutes and I've done it thousands of times, but now it feels both new and reassuringly familiar. It's as if, when the bandages were removed from my eyes, a veil has also been ripped from my mind. Everything seems so clear and beautiful.

I feel happy, even under these difficult circumstances and I can tell my happiness is being picked up by Mom. She's humming to herself, her face relaxed and calm.

Fatcat is waiting at the front door when we arrive. I've forgotten all about him but he hasn't forgotten about me. Nor my role as chief food provider.

My ankles are bleeding by the time I get past him to the kitchen, Mom laughing at the sight of me trying to fend off an angry cat.

"Serves you right," she says. "That cat is *never* going to be a house cat. He's feral and he's only with you for the food. You don't provide that, he's going to let you know he's unhappy."

"Ya think?"

The can opener isn't working fast enough for

Fatcat but this time I anticipate his attack and manage to get my ankles out of the way before he does more damage. The cat food disappears in a moment.

Fatcat transforms himself into a regular cat, curling around my bleeding ankles and purring. I reach down to pet him, but he's having none of that.

"What am I going to do with you, Fatcat? I can't take you over to Mom's, it'll drive you crazy, all the noise and people and excitement."

Fatcat and I are alike in that way. I'd love to just come home to my house and take a day to figure out everything that's happened to me since Carrick Jones first walked into my life. But I can't.

"I'll be back after dinner," I say to Fatcat and to the part of myself who just wants a little alone time.

"Mom," I yell down the stairs, "I'm going to get changed. The box is on the bookshelf in my office." I don't know why I tell her, she obviously knows already, but I guess I feel as though I'm giving her permission.

I sit down at the desk in my bedroom and hesitate, just for a moment, before I touch Lisa Martin's photograph. I don't want her to die, not now we've found her. I can see the outline of her face though I can't yet make out details.

I hesitate, again, and then lightly lay my hand

over her face, and wait. Nothing. Not a tingle. Not a jolt. Not anything.

What if they rescued her and she died on the way to the hospital? What if they rescued her and she died on the operating table? What if she died before she could see her family again? What if?

There are a million what-ifs involved in my gift and I'm used to them. At least I should be. Because every single time someone walks away from my house I go through the same list.

What if they're already dead?

What if they don't want to be found?

What if nothing changes?

The list is part of the gift for me, the what-ifs part of the penance I pay for not having a strong enough gift to save anyone.

"She's in intensive care," Mom says when I get back down the stairs, Lisa Martin's photograph tucked carefully into my pocket and the radio playing in the background. "But they think she's going to be okay. She's got broken bones, hypothermia, but the biggest problem is dehydration. Luckily she had just been to the store and had water in the front seat with her."

I breathe a sigh of relief, knowing that my obsession with Lisa Martin's fate won't go away, knowing that every day for the rest of my life I'm going to be checking up on her because I saved her.

She's the first one, the only one I know for sure, and I won't give up on her. I don't know that I'll be able to save her again, but if I check every day, at least I'll know.

Jim is pulling into the driveway just as we arrive back at Mom's house. He has a briefcase full of paper. I hand him my little index box and he laughs.

"Nice filing system you have," he says, "are they at least in alphabetical order?"

I cringe. Of course they're not in alphabetical order, that would mean thinking of my gift as a business, and it's not. I just write down what I hear and put the card in the box.

"It's more a chronological system," I say, trying to sound as if it's a system I chose rather than a default plan.

"Okay, well, I've brought the alphabetical list I had the office prepare, but it won't have all the information on the cards."

"That's how I'll know who they are. I don't remember the names, but I might remember the stories."

Aunt Lucy and Mom are sitting around the dining room table. It's a room we use rarely, choosing almost always to eat in the bright kitchen. But the table is huge, plenty of room for Uncle Jim's files and for all of us.

Mom has turned on the lights but even though it's not yet dark outside, this room is always gloomy. The windows face north and the tall pines at the property line block what little light there is.

Uncle Jim puts down the files and the index box and looks at them. He shuffles the files, then pulls a stapled list from the top one.

"Okay, I think we can work with my lists for now, and eliminate all of the women who visited Ria."

"But…" Mom hesitates. She doesn't want to say whatever it is in front of me.

"Mom, just say it."

"What if it's one of their husbands? Or brothers or fathers? I mean, it could be anyone."

"But why would someone want to hurt me? And why would one of my clients kill Frank Morrison?"

Uncle Jim snorts. "First of all, why do you think it's the same person? And I can think of a dozen reasons why someone—either one of your clients or one of their family members—would want to hurt you."

Aunt Lucy and Mom nod which means that they can think of reasons why someone I tried to help would want to hurt me. Damn.

It's great that I can see their faces, really it is, but I think this conversation might be easier if I couldn't. I'm not sure I want to know any of Jim's reasons, and I'm pretty sure I don't want to be having this discussion.

So I answer Uncle Jim's first question. "Too much of a coincidence. Nothing happened to me for almost thirty years and then all of this stuff at the same time? I can't believe it's unrelated."

They nod again, and this time Uncle Jim joins them.

"Okay," he says. "Let's get going."

It takes us several hours, including a break for dinner which I don't enjoy as much as I thought I would, to cross reference the lists. We have forty names, none of which mean a thing to me.

"We'll do the index cards tomorrow." I'm so tired I can't concentrate anymore and the rest of them look worse than I do.

"I'll drop you off on my way home," Jim says. "I'll pick you up in the morning, too."

I can hardly wait until I can drive again. I hate being dependent on someone else for transportation. The good news is that I can shop—at least at stores within walking distance—I can cook and clean and sit on my porch and watch the world go by.

"I have to do some things at home, so can we make it after lunch?"

I don't tell them, but all I really want is some time to spend with Fatcat and my house and myself. Some time to think about what's happening and why and how I'm going to solve all these problems before I have to go back to work.

And especially some time to think about what I'm going to do about Carrick Jones.

CHAPTER 20

The house settles around me like a pair of comfortable slippers. I'm not happy but I'm content and my vision seems to be improving all the time. Things out at the outer edge—like the walls—are a bit blurry but the close up things are perfectly clear.

And right close up to me is Lisa Martin's photograph. She's still alive and she's not going to die—at least not soon. I know she's alive because I heard it on the news a few minutes ago; I know she's not going to die because…

I know she's not going to die because of my gift. There is nothing at all when I touch her photograph. And though my gift has shifted over the past few days, I know that the basics still work.

I can't be sure about the add-ons. I don't know if I'll ever feel what hit me with Lisa's picture when I *knew* she was near Oak Heights. And I'm pretty sure I'll never feel what I felt when I shook

Frank Morrison's hand. I think my fainting spells are over.

But, given the givens of my gift, I suspect that those changes weren't permanent, that they were given to me because I needed them. And maybe what I'll have—until the problem is solved—is some version of them.

Will I still be able to see death in the Yellow Pages? Will I ever do it again? No. Too much responsibility and way too much stress.

I'm not even sure I want to keep *any* of these changes to my gift. I know I've wished to save someone. And I have. Lisa Martin.

But saving one person makes me want to save them all. And I can't. No matter what I do, how many hours, how much energy, I devote to my gift, I'll never be able to save everyone.

Now I understand how Carrick Jones feels about working homicide. There are too many people he can't save and it's eating him up inside.

The phone rings and even though it isn't my gift telling me, I do know that Carrick is at the other end of the phone. I hesitate through two rings and then pick it up.

"Carrick? Is she going to be okay?"

"She's going to live."

It's obvious that he has chosen his words very carefully, that she might not be okay. I wait for the rest.

"The doctors say that if she'd been there even one more day, she would have died. They're amazed that she's still alive, and they're doing everything they can to save her. She's going to lose her right leg. It broke in the accident and... Well, that's all they know for sure."

The stress in his voice is painful to hear. "Carrick? Have you eaten? Why don't you come over here and I'll heat up Mom's leftovers?"

"Are you there by yourself?"

I've forgotten he doesn't know I went to the doctor this morning, doesn't know that I can see again. I hesitate before I speak. Is he more likely to come over if I can or if I can't see?

"I got the bandages off this morning." I don't say anything else but leave the decision to him.

His hesitation is slightly longer than mine. "I've still got some work to do here. Is an hour okay?" he asks. "What's for dinner?"

"Pork roast, scalloped potatoes, green beans. Apple pie for dessert."

"Make that half an hour."

I'm certain this is the first almost-ordinary conversation we've had since the Friday night he and Frank Morrison showed up at my door.

Fatcat and the kitchen go together. He's under the table while I unpack the leftovers and put them in pans—some in the oven, some on the stovetop. He's purring and I wonder if he's happy that I'm home and not tripping over him, if he's sensed that I'll be here for a while, feeding him regularly.

I set the table with my favorite plates, a deep rich blue with a brilliant red stripe around the edge. I add wine glasses and open a bottle of Côtes du Rhône from the stash in the basement.

Candles next, the same blue as the plates. The sun is just at the horizon but I light the candles anyway, mostly because I want to see them flicker in the darkening evening.

The room begins to fill with aromas—the dusty smell of an oven that hasn't been used for a while, the sensual scent of the wine breathing, the saliva-inducing smell of the warming food. Underneath it all, I sense more than smell Fatcat, his cat-ness, a combination of wildness, warmth and laziness.

If I hadn't been there when the window broke, I wouldn't have known anything had happened to it. Whoever Carrick called did a great job of replacing it, the blinds matching perfectly. Now I need to run upstairs and check on the blinds in my bedroom. I forgot to look when I was in there this afternoon, concentrating fiercely on Lisa's photograph and seeing nothing else.

Those blinds, too, have been replaced, though not by Carrick and not quite as perfectly. They're a shade lighter than the ones on the other windows, a permanent reminder to me to be more careful, to move more slowly, to think about what I'm doing before I leap right in and do it.

But tonight I'm going to take another leap. One that will, I hope, take me right into the arms of Carrick Jones.

And this isn't about what it is we need to do together, it's not about the work, it's about how I imagine it's going to feel, the two of us together. Being blind has given me plenty of time to dream about it, to imagine the feel of his body on mine, the taste of his skin and the touch of his hands.

There's a light knock at the back door but he doesn't wait for me to open it, he just steps in.

I've forgotten what he looks like, I realize, over the past days. I've forgotten how tall he is, how solid and sure of himself he appears. I had this picture of him in my mind, but as the days progressed, the picture got hazy and what I saw was mostly about his voice.

Carrick Jones has the voice of a blues singer, deep and ragged and sorrowful. But he has the body of an angel. At least the kind of angel I'd want to make love with. He's big all over, big hands and face and arms. Nothing of him is small or namby-pamby. He's all male.

Today he looks tired but content, the lines on his face deep and strong, permanent lines. Whatever stress fractures he's been carrying since I've met him are gone temporarily, replaced by a layer of peace I suspect he doesn't wear very often. His shoulders and hands are relaxed and he smiles at me.

"Any new injuries I should know about?" he asks as he moves across the room to where I'm sitting.

"Nope, and some of the old ones are healing." I gesture at my face and wonder if he has remembered what I look like under the bandages. And then I realize that it doesn't matter because he remembers *me*.

He stops for a minute as he passes the stove, stops to turn off the oven and the burner. He stops again to pick up the bottle of wine and the wine glasses. He doesn't stop as he passes me, just assumes I'll follow him up the stairs. And he's right. I do.

The water in my giant tub is running by the time I make it up the stairs and the candles I always have in the bathroom are lit. His clothes are in a messy pile beside the door and I hear him splashing as he steps into the tub.

I smile, then shiver as I carefully tug off my shirt, and then the bandages on my arms. The cuts themselves don't hurt, but there's still an ache under them, and the bruising is starting to show. I ignore them, pull off my bra, my jeans, my panties and step into the room, buck naked.

The glasses sparkle in the candlelight, the crimson wine shooting sparks of color around the room. I stand in the doorway and enjoy what I see, everything I see.

Carrick's eyes are closed, his big body settled into the warm water as if it belongs there, as if it's been waiting for this moment for a very long time. He smiles when he hears me, but he doesn't open his eyes, he just lifts his hand to help me into the tub.

The water's exactly the right temperature, hot enough that it stings when I step into it, but not too hot that the hurt lasts more than a few moments.

My skin tingles as I slide down into the water, slide against Carrick's body, already warmed by the water. He waits until I'm sitting in the tub, my body between his legs, my head against his chest, before handing me a glass of wine.

I close my eyes and take a sip of the wine, smooth and fragrant against my tongue. I feel more than hear his voice when he speaks.

"Can we just leave everything for tonight? No complications, no problems?"

I smile, knowing he can't see me. "Yes. Please," I say, because I don't want anything to spoil this night. We're more in harmony than we've ever been and I want us to stay there.

Just for this one night, I promise, and push the thoughts of Morrison and the client list from my mind to concentrate on the man and this moment.

The slow pressure of his hands on my body, the rush of cool air as we step out of the tub into the dark bedroom, the anticipation…

Days and days and nights of anticipation.

None of my imaginings come close to the real thing. Carrick has slow hands and an uncanny sense of what I need, what we both need, and he takes me to places I've never been, places I've never imagined, until I can't breathe, can only feel.

No words are spoken or needed. Touch and taste and deep caresses are enough for this night. In the hours of darkness, we forge a new entity. We become one in the way I've dreamed of and I know that nothing can damage that connection.

BUT THE COMING OF the morning, as it has for most of my life, brings with it the concerns of the real world. We made love in the darkness, the candles having sputtered to their death by the time we left the bath. Our other senses heightened by the absence of sight, we spent those hours wrapped in each other.

It's late for me, and I expect for Carrick as well, when we finally wake and stay that way. The room is dark and still—I can't sleep if there's any light at all—but this morning I see his face on the pillow next to mine. It's all I want, I think.

But of course it's not.

This connection we've forged can't, won't, be broken, but there is too much for us to worry about to enjoy it the way we should. Last night's hours were out of time, and now we have to return to the worries of this complicated world we live in.

The shower's running when I open the blinds. I wonder whether I'll still be able to sense my watcher now that I can see and I test it. Not a very valid test because if he's not there I won't feel him even if it's still possible for me. I don't feel anything.

I use the bathroom down the hall and meet Carrick in the kitchen, following the scent of coffee to find him. He's sitting at the kitchen table, all the doors and windows open, coffee steaming in two cups on the table.

"Cream, right?" he says, handing me a cup when I sit down, his hand lingering on mine.

In the brilliant light of the morning, I check his face. No signs of regret, simply contentment and an unlikely twist of humor. He grins at my scrutiny.

"No regrets," he says, "it would have happened before if I'd been myself." A small twinge of pain crosses his eyes and he shakes it away. "You?"

"No. Not a single one. The only regret I have is that it's morning and there are things I have to tell you."

"Oh, surprise," he laughs. "Can we eat first?"

We work well together in the kitchen, no bumps or awkwardness. I take that as another sign that this is right, that we've made the right decision, if you can call something as inevitable as this a decision.

Bacon, eggs, hashbrowns, orange juice and another pot of coffee later, we clear off the table and Carrick says, "Okay, I'm ready."

CHAPTER 21

"Someone is trying to hurt me."

Carrick glares at the cuts and bruising on my arms and the dark glasses I'm wearing. "You're kidding," he says, "I hadn't noticed."

I ignore his sarcasm though I can't help grinning even though his brows have lowered over his eyes, hiding their expression, but the heaviness of the lines around them say it all. He's considering my statement.

Everything that's happened crosses his face— Frank Morrison, my fainting spells, the accident which wasn't one and blinded me, the watcher—as whatever humor he'd felt at the idea disappears. By the time he's finished, he looks as if he's swallowed a mouthful of poison.

Because he believes me, because there's too much evidence to deny, because Lisa Martin wasn't kidnapped, and because I helped him save her.

"It has to be someone who's come to me for help," I say. "It can't be anyone else."

I watch as he thinks about that, his lips pursing while he cycles that through his cop's brain. He nods and I continue.

"And it has to be someone who had access to the Marathon site."

He nods again, this time more quickly. He's still not talking, which worries me a bit, but I carry on as if he's completely with me.

"We spent yesterday going through the lists. Uncle Jim's list of all my clients…"

Carrick wants to say something, but he stops himself, and waits. There's that cop patience, let the victim or the suspect tell the story. Let the silence entice them into revealing more than they would otherwise.

"I know what you're doing," I say, "but it's okay. I'm going to tell you the whole thing anyway."

He grins in acknowledgement but still doesn't speak. When Carrick grins he's irresistible and I don't try to resist him. I lean over, moving his coffee cup from between us, take his face in my hands and kiss him.

It starts out as a you're-killing-me-you-idiot kind of kiss but it quickly turns into something else, something deeper and warmer and far more satisfying. It almost turns into a quick trip back upstairs but he stops, pulling back before it goes so far neither of us can stop it.

"Tell me," he whispers against my hair, "tell me everything. What list? And what are you comparing it to?"

So I tell him. I tell him about my box of index cards. I tell him about my family's worry and their ongoing plans to keep me safe. I tell him about Uncle Jim's list of my clients and his list of Marathon workers.

I tell him that the watcher followed me again the other day. He frowns at that but waits for me to finish.

I save the worst for last.

"I think Frank Morrison was killed because of me. I think it's someone who's been watching me, someone who panicked when he saw police officers show up at my house. I don't know why anyone would do that, but we all think that there has to be some overlap between my clients and someone at Marathon. So we're starting there."

Carrick doesn't say anything yet, but I know that he's gone right to the heart of the problem. Why Frank Morrison? Why not Carrick Jones?

"There's one more link we're going to have to make," Carrick says, finally breaking his silence. "He murdered Frank, not me. That means, whatever it is, there's a connection somewhere to Frank as well. When we find someone who connects to all three of you—Ria, Frank, the Marathon worksite—we'll have our killer."

"How are we going to do that?"

"I don't know yet," Carrick says, sweeping me off my chair and into his arms, "but let's worry about it later."

"CALL YOUR MOTHER." Carrick rolls over and hands me the phone. "We might as well work at their place."

Fatcat is purring at the bottom of the bed. He likes Carrick better than he likes me, that's for sure. He's never once slept on the bed before this.

Maybe he recognizes Carrick's innate protectiveness, maybe he knows, like I do, that he's safe with Carrick, that no one will dare harm him while Carrick's around.

"I'll drop you off and run down to the station. I want to compare Frank's cases with your lists. Maybe we'll find a connection."

I make the phone call. Mom's fretting and she's cooking a turkey with all the fixings. It doesn't matter if it's the middle of the summer, but when she's really worried, she cooks turkey.

I pass the information along to Carrick. He grins.

"I could get used to this." He runs his hand over my naked body. "You. Your mom's cooking. Even Fatcat."

"Good," I say, "because none of us will give you up, you know. You're stuck with us for the duration."

"I know." And his eyes shine with promises I know he'll keep. "What time's dinner?"

"Time for you to have a shower and get to the station. I'll meet you at home. Hurry," I say, not wanting him to leave, not wanting to drive over there by myself.

"We'll shower together, and then I'll drop you off." He pulls me out of bed and hurries me into the shower. "No hanky panky, either. We don't have time."

I don't know whether he's picked up my fear but he gets out of the car when he stops in front of the house and walks me up to the door, kissing me, hard, before pushing me inside.

"Stay," is on my lips but I don't say it. We need to resolve this because I hate being scared.

Now that I see the sunlight, the trees, the faces of the people around me, my gift has blurred back to its old level, like a sense-enhancing drug has been flushed from my system.

"He's coming back for dinner." Gran states as if there's no question about it.

I head for the kitchen, Gran toddling along after

me. Uncle Jim, Aunt Lucy and Mom are all there and they're drinking red wine. I pour myself a glass and settle in for the inquisition.

It's not as painful as I expect. They don't want details—thank God, because I blush just thinking about some of those details—but they do want to know that Carrick understands what it all means. Yes, I keep saying, yes, he feels the same way. Yes, he's going to stick around. No, we haven't talked about marriage. And yes, he'll be back for dinner.

We haven't really talked about anything except the connections we need to make between Frank Morrison and my lists. But there's no question in my mind or my heart as I answer their questions just as I'm sure there are no questions in Carrick's. This is it for both of us.

If we can just solve this one small problem that surrounds us.

"He's gone to pick up Frank Morrison's files," I tell them once they're satisfied about Carrick's intentions. "Because…"

Uncle Jim, as always, catches on immediately. "Because that's the third point of the triangle. Why Frank Morrison and not Carrick? Because Frank knew something or someone. Frank showing up at your house was what started all this."

I try not to think about the thing that's been worrying me ever since Carrick and I had this conversation in my kitchen. But what if it's *not* Frank? What if it's Frank *and* Carrick?

We move into the dining room and dig once more into the lists. There are no overlaps, no people on Uncle Jim's list who show up on the Marathon list.

"Do you have pictures?" I ask, finally putting down the two lists in despair.

"I have the applications for every single person who's applied at Marathon over the past year. The people who got jobs have identity photos. They're clipped to the applications."

I don't ask how Uncle Jim got the original applications and photos. He knows pretty much everybody in this city and pretty much every person he knows owes him a favor or two. Some of them probably more than that. Someone in the personnel department at Marathon must have owed Uncle Jim big time.

"Let's pull out everybody who ever worked—even if only as a day laborer—on my job site. Maybe I'll recognize one of them."

It's going to be hard enough looking at just those photos. There are probably fifty full-time guys and another fifty or so day laborers. And then there are the people who quit, including my welding crew.

For a woman who avoids photographs unless she's forced to see them by clients, these past weeks have been photo central. I rub the hard edges of the photo of Lisa Martin that I'm carrying in my pocket.

"More wine?" I ask, holding up my empty glass. They nod and turn back to the applications.

I have to sit down to do this. Gran has followed me into the kitchen but she's puttering around in the refrigerator—snacks, I'll bet—and she's the only person that won't find anything strange about me looking at a photograph. She finds very little strange anymore.

Lisa Martin looks so happy in the photograph, so full of life. I touch the photograph right at the edge of her left cheek where it's turned grubby from my fingers. Nothing.

I've been so engrossed in Lisa Martin that I didn't hear Carrick arrive, but when I return to the dining room with the bottle of wine, he's there, conferring at the head of the table with Uncle Jim.

They're having a discussion about how to compare the lists. Carrick's not too keen on anybody else looking at Frank's list of cases, but Uncle Jim, as always, wins the battle.

"It'll go faster if we all do it," he says, and in the end, that's the argument that convinces Jones.

"Do I need to look at the photos?" I ask, grabbing

another glass out of the china cabinet and handing it, filled with wine, to Carrick.

"What photos?" Carrick holds my hand for a minute, then raises it to his lips. His look asks, "are you okay?" and I nod.

"Um, well, those photos are a bit tricky," Mom says.

"They're not tricky at all," Uncle Jim interjects. "I got them legitimately."

"Of course you did," Mom replies but her tone of voice says she knows the truth.

"Tell me about the photos." Carrick's calm voice cuts through the argument like a hot knife through white pudding.

Absent-mindedly, I wonder if Aunt Lucy has made her famous white pudding and caramel sauce to go with the fruit cake. We *never* have turkey, even in the middle of the summer, without fruit cake, white pudding and caramel sauce.

"I have applications from Marathon. Those who got jobs have identity photos. Copies are clipped to the forms."

"Ah," Carrick grins. "I get the picture."

"Ha, ha," I say, "very funny. Let's get on with this, okay? We've only got an hour before dinner."

The hour passes, Mom and Aunt Lucy occasionally dipping out to stir something, baste the turkey, turn on or off another element on the stove. The smell of turkey has permeated the entire house and my mouth is watering.

By the end of it, we're no further ahead than we were before, except for another bottle of wine, and the fact that I haven't yet had to look at the photographs.

We don't have a single name that is on all three lists. We don't have a single name that is even on two of the lists.

"Now what?" I ask, leaning back in my chair.

Carrick moves his chair next to mine and puts his arm around my shoulders, his big warm hand massaging my neck. "The photos," he says, "but not until after dinner."

CHAPTER 22

Sated and slightly tipsy, we slowly return to the dining room and the photographs.

"I don't know if I can do this with all of you around."

"Of course you can." Aunt Lucy's usually crisp tones are rounded at the edges by food and wine. "You've done it in restaurants and school corridors, for heaven's sake."

I'm just trying to postpone the inevitable. I don't want to look at a hundred photographs. I especially don't want to do it in front of Carrick Jones.

I don't have any idea how I'll react to these photographs. I haven't tried, except with Lisa Martin and the Yellow Pages. I *really* don't want to faint. Or have some kind of fit.

"Pass me the applications," I finally say, taking another sip of wine to fortify myself.

There's nothing, not even a mild tingle, from the first pile of photographs. And for first time I can remember, I feel like a normal person, just looking at pictures. I've never looked at a bunch of pictures together, never gone through friends' vacation snapshots, never looked at someone's wedding album. But this feels kind of normal.

"Hand me the next pile."

Again, nothing. And now I'm beginning to worry. Not that I've lost my gift, but because I don't recognize any of them and some of these men worked with me every single day over the past months. And I don't know their faces.

They're terrible photographs. Even I, who never looks at photographs, can see that. But you'd think I'd know one of them. I clutch Carrick's hand even tighter before I nod at Uncle Jim to hand me the last bunch of applications.

"It's okay, Ria," Carrick whispers. "This was a long shot, anyway."

I smile crookedly at him. "A long shot, but the only shot we've got," I say, reaching for another pile of applications.

"Not the only shot. I told the chief I was taking a leave of absence this morning."

"What?" I shot up out of my chair. "A leave of absence?"

"He's been after me to do it ever since Frank. But

I wanted to find Lisa Martin and you did that for me. So I'm just doing what he told me to do.

"But it means I can stay with you, make sure you're okay. At least until we find this guy. So don't worry if you don't find anything," he leans in closer, "I'll keep you safe."

"But I have to go back to work."

"Not until we find this guy." Mom, Aunt Lucy and Jim speak in unison. Mom continues, "You can't go back to work until we find him. What if next time…"

Next time. I try not to think of what might happen the next time, try to blot out the picture I've been carrying around in my head of Frank Morrison lying dead in the alley.

"Okay," I say, "So hand me the damned applications and let's see if we can find this guy."

Carrick's hand is still on my shoulder and the tickle of his breath on my neck reminds me of the other benefits to this leave of absence.

The final set of photographs tell me nothing. Not the slightest twinge, either from the gift or of recognition.

"Uncle Jim, are you sure these are people who've worked at my job site?" I can't believe I don't recognize a single one of them.

"Yes, though I can't be sure about the day laborers.

Not all of them have photos or even applications. Sometimes they just pick them up from a street corner or a coffee shop."

"But I don't know any of them."

Carrick's hand runs down my arm to my hand and holds it. "These are terrible photographs, even worse than drivers' licenses, and I thought those were the worst."

"So what do we do now?"

"We start from the source material. Your index cards. You said yourself that all Jim took from there was the names. Maybe something else you wrote will remind you of something."

I'd told Carrick on the way over that the index cards were only impressions. I put down their names, though the spelling was probably suspect. But more importantly, I included how they seemed to be feeling. Why they wanted to find their lost loved ones. Where they came from. How they reacted when I gave them the news. Or the news that there was no news.

"But none of the names match."

"People change their names. And maybe it's not one of the people who came to see you, but a relative, a friend, an associate. There are all kinds of reasons that the names won't work."

Carrick hesitates. "Maybe," he says, slowly and

carefully, "maybe you can read the cards the way you read photographs."

I look down at our entwined hands and see that their embrace isn't just physical, it's much more than that. We've become partners in a much larger way. Because now he believes in my gift, maybe even more than I do right now.

"I don't know if it's changed that much."

"Can't hurt to try, can it?"

The rest of the family nods their approval.

"Okay," I say, "I'll do it but don't expect anything. I don't."

The index cards are all different colors and all different sizes. At the beginning, I figured I wouldn't need many so I bought a single package. Plain white ones. No lines. One hundred cards.

That first package of cards lasted a long time, maybe two or three years. But as the years progressed, I had to buy a new package of cards more often.

I bought fluorescent pink ones. Blue ones. Yellow ones. I bought bigger ones. Smaller ones. Ones with lines. Ones with designs on the front and a place for a recipe on the back.

There is no system to the cards except that the oldest ones are at the front and the newest ones at the back. Mostly.

They're written in pencil, in blue and black and red ink. Sometimes even in green or purple ink, depending on what was handy at that time.

Sometimes I printed the names and the few notes underneath it, sometimes I wrote them. Occasionally, if I was feeling extra organized or bored, I typed them on the computer and then printed them out. I never saved the notes to the hard drive, though, because I had a feeling about the index cards.

They reminded me of the old card catalogues in libraries, the annotated ones, with notes going back years and years and years. They felt personal, and the index cards still feel that way to me. I think I *need* them to be personal.

And maybe Carrick's right, maybe I will be able to read the cards. "Where do I start?"

Everyone looks at each other and all of us shrug. Uncle Jim finally speaks, "When did Frank become a police officer? It won't be before that."

This is what I love about Uncle Jim. It doesn't matter that he's almost eighty, he's still the most logical, most practical person I know.

"He joined the department five years before me. That'll be seventeen years ago."

"Okay." I grab the box of cards from the center of the table and I shuffle through all of the white cards, and part of the fluorescent pink ones. "There aren't always dates, but I remember some of them. These ones were before Frank joined for sure."

Carrick takes a quick look at the table. "Ria, move over here." He points at a chair next to the china cabinet. "Lucy, turn on that lamp." He points to the lamp in the cabinet. "Jim, Gran, Mom," no one even blinks at his use of those names, "sit over here."

Suddenly, I'm on one side of the table, lit up like an all-night grocery store, and everyone else except Carrick is across the room from me. It kind of feels like an interrogation, or it would if Carrick weren't sitting next to me.

"All of you, I want you to watch Ria carefully. You've seen her do this before and she might give you a sign that she's not aware of. Anything unusual, anything that clicks for you, stop her."

He pulls my chair closer to his, until we're sitting thigh to thigh, shoulder to shoulder. "I'll be right here. Just try it, okay? If it doesn't work, we'll think of something else."

The room, silent except for our breathing and the tick-tick of the wall clock, closes in around me until all I see are Carrick's hands on the table next to me and the cards he's pulled from the box.

"Start here," he says, and hands me a small pile

of cards, maybe twenty or thirty. The ones at the front of the pile are pink, then they shift to pale blue. "Read them. Touch them, one at a time. If you feel anything, stop."

"Okay." But I feel stupid. I have no idea what might happen.

Mostly what happens is nothing. I go through the first pile of cards. I read the notes from seventeen years ago and they are as new to me as they must be to Carrick when he takes what I've discarded and reads them after me.

"Nothing," I mutter, taking each card separately and holding it in my hands before I read the names and the notes. "Nothing," I whisper, wondering if any of these people are still alive and if they remember the day they went to that crazy lady who sees death.

"Nothing," I say again, picking up a purple card with white flowers embossed in the top right hand corner, and remembering the face of a young girl who'd lost her twin sister.

Her name was Marylou, her sister's Maryjean. They'd grown up in foster care, a good place, Marylou said, but Maryjean hated everything about it. So when she turned eighteen—two years ago, Marylou said at the time—she took off. *She's not dead*, Marylou repeated, time and again, *she's not dead because I'd know it if she were. But something's wrong, something big.*

She looks just like me, Marylou said, *we're identical. That's how I'd know if something happened to her, just like she'd know if something happened to me. We've always known. Here's a picture of her.*

She handed me a snapshot of a girl who looked exactly like the young woman sitting in front of me, except the girl in the photograph wasn't wringing her hands and her eyes weren't darkened with sorrow. *She's been okay so far, that's why I haven't tried too hard to find her. If she wanted me, she knows where I am. I haven't moved, still have the same job. She's been okay*, she repeated, as if to excuse her neglect.

I knew the minute I touched the photograph that her sister was going to die. And for the first time in a long time, I didn't want to tell her the truth.

But she saw it in my face before I could decide what to do.

She's going to die, isn't she? She turned her face away for a moment. *I knew it. I'm going to find her*, she said. *Thank you. Now I can find her before it happens.*

I haven't said any of this out loud and I don't think I feel anything except the sorrow of Marylou, but Carrick puts his hand down on mine before I can give him the card.

"What is it?"

Mom and Uncle Jim, Lucy and Gran watch me, cautiously, from the other side of the table. I know I haven't done anything unusual, no blackouts, no weird sounds uttering from my mouth, no weirdness at all.

But they think I have.

Carrick asks again, "Ria, angel, what is it?"

"Nothing," I say.

CHAPTER 23

But it isn't nothing.

It isn't me who figures it out, though, it's Carrick. He takes the card from my hand and says, "Tell us the story, Ria. Who is," he looks down at the card in his hands, "Marylou Scott?"

His brows meet between his eyes for a moment, a puzzled look that doesn't bode well for whatever it is I'm going to tell him. But I tell him anyway.

I tell the family about Marylou and her sister Maryjean. I tell them everything I know, which isn't much. Not really. I tell them that I don't know where she's from, except that it's somewhere close by.

"How do you know that?" Carrick voices the question everyone else won't ask.

"Because she said she was going to find her sister. And she'd have to find her fast. She didn't have time to drive out of state or fly across the country if she was going to find Maryjean. It had to be close."

"God," Carrick says, "I never even thought of people who don't live in this city." He runs his hands through his hair, stroking his scalp as if to rid himself of a headache.

I stop him, placing my hands over his, rubbing my thumbs over his temple. *Don't worry*, I say to him without speaking, *don't worry like this*.

Uncle Jim once again solves the problem. "If any one of Ria's people was from out of town, there couldn't be a connection to Frank. So it wouldn't matter. Don't need to worry about those folks."

The tension I'm feeling in Carrick's temples and brows is gone. Don't need to worry about those folks. But what about all the ones when I didn't know where they were from, or where I thought it didn't matter? What about all of them?

I can't change the past, can't change the way I did things, and probably won't change the way I do this in the future. At least I have the cards. At least they go back far enough. At least I have the names.

"This is the one," Carrick says, suddenly jumping from his chair and heading around the other side of the table. "I'm sure of it."

He grabs for Frank's list and runs his finger over it. Marylou," he mutters, "Maryjean. It's not Scott.

That's not how it's listed, but I know it's here. I know I saw it."

The only sound in the room is the tick-tick of the clock, the soft sounds of breathing, and Carrick's mumble. "It's here, I know it's here."

Uncle Jim gets up from his chair. "Give me half of the list, Carrick."

"Hell. No need. I've found it, found them." He sounds exhausted, as if the mere words were too much for him.

"Ria, can you give me a date for Marylou's visit? Even a guess?"

"Give me back the card. If I put it back in its place, I may be able to tell. Some of the cards around it probably have dates. Or I might remember when one of them appeared, you know, if it was a holiday or a birthday or something."

I tuck Marylou's card back in where it belongs and read, again, the cards in front of and behind it. They don't tell me much, there are no dates, but when I read the card two places after Marylou's I know exactly when it was.

The same week Mama Amata died.

That's why the details are so sketchy. I was too stressed and too tired to do more than look at photographs and write down the names. I'm surprised I remember Marylou as clearly as I do.

"When did Mama Amata die?"

"Fourteen years ago in March. March 21. I remember it because it was the first day of spring and we were all so sad. And it was a miserable day, sleet and hail and a vicious wind. We felt like spring would never come again." Gran leans against Uncle Jim as if she were experiencing that pain over again.

"She's right," I say to Carrick. "That's why I didn't want to tell Marylou about her sister. I'd seen enough pain for one week."

He turns the page of the list and stops, his finger on an entry halfway down. *It's there*, I think, *the connection*. Uncle Jim was right. Carrick was right. *I* was right. *This is about me.*

"I have to go back to the station," he says. "I need to get the file from storage. Wait for me here," he kisses my cheek. "Don't go out."

He turns to the rest of the family. "No matter what she offers you, do not let her leave this house. And don't any of you go anywhere with her. It's too dangerous. I'll be back as soon as I can."

The warmth in the room disappears with him. Before I can reach it, Uncle Jim has grabbed the page and brings it over to my side of the table where the light is.

"Oh," he says, "I remember now."

Gran totters over to him and puts her arms around his waist. "What is it? What do you remember?"

"We should wait for Carrick to get back." I know he's saying that because he doesn't want to tell us the story, it's too painful, but I'm not going to wait.

"Tell us."

It's all I say but he succumbs immediately, slumping into a chair with all the bonelessness of a sleepy child.

"Sit down," he says first, "all of you sit down. It's not nice. I know you've guessed that, but I don't expect you've guessed just how bad it is."

Lucy pulls Uncle Jim to his feet and tugs him toward the kitchen. "If we're going to hear something terrible, let's do it in the kitchen."

When we're all seated around the brightly lit and polished table in the kitchen, surrounded by the smells of turkey dinner and lavender-scented dishwashing liquid, clean glasses and a bottle of Cabernet in front of us, Jim begins.

"I'm sure they didn't have the last name of Scott," he says, "because I'd remember that, I think. It was—" he pauses to dig into his memory "—something much more memorable, because it always sounded to me like they didn't belong here. Messier. That's what it was.

"They didn't find the bodies for a few days, and then only because one of the other tenants smelled them."

He ignores the cringes from around the table and carries on with the story. "Two girls, twins they were, both battered to death on the bathroom floor. What was weird about it was that they hadn't been killed at the same time. One was dead maybe a day or two before the other."

"Maryjean," I whisper. "She died before her sister could get to her."

"Maryjean," Uncle Jim agrees. "She'd been dead for at least a day before Marylou. Maryjean looked like she was killed in a fit of rage, but Marylou, well, let's just say that her last hours weren't good ones."

The picture in my head is too accurate for comfort. I've seen way too many serial killer movies not to know what torture looks like.

"Who did it?" Mom breaks the spell I'm under, asking the question, pouring more wine into my glass, touching my arm as she sits back.

"No one knows. Maryjean had a boyfriend but they never found him. The cops tried everything—rewards, *America's Most Wanted*. Every year for five or six years after it happened, the news shows and papers had an update. Never any additional information, but they didn't forget those girls for quite a while. They didn't have any family, so that made it harder. Sometimes it felt like the whole city mourned them like sisters."

"How does he know about me?"

"That's the reason he tortured Marylou," Carrick says, returning with a banker's box and bringing the chill of the evening into the kitchen with him. "He wanted to know how she found Maryjean."

"You can't know that."

"No, but it makes sense. And that's how he knows about you. He's probably been watching you on and off ever since."

"What about Frank?"

"He was lead on the case. It was a case that nagged him over all the years I knew him, that he hadn't caught the bastard who killed those girls. But now we've got a shot at it."

Carrick looks as if he's been given a second lease on life, a way to make everything right for Frank Morrison. Determined, angry, and in a hurry.

"How?"

"Because he must be on the Marathon list. And I'm willing to bet you that within a few months after he killed those girls, he showed up at your place for a reading. And I'll bet he brought a picture of the twins with him."

"Oh my God, you're right. There was a man…"

I don't have to go to the dining room to get the cards, Mom's already brought them to me. I scrabble through the index cards, throwing the ones with female names down on the table, holding the others in my suddenly sweaty palm.

"It can't be too long after I saw Marylou, not years or anything."

"No," Carrick agrees, "he wouldn't want to wait that long to find out what you knew, what you might find out about him. He'd want to know if you knew about the murders. I mean, you'd sent Marylou to find her sister."

I take the dozen or so cards I've pulled from the box. "Carrick," I order, "get the lists. Give them to Mom and Aunt Lucy and Jim. Take part of them for yourself. See if any of these names are on any of the lists."

Of course they weren't. Not one of the names I held in my hands were on any of the lists.

"Ria," says Uncle Jim, "he has to be a big man. Think about Frank, think about the machete."

I do, though yet again it's a picture I wish I

couldn't see. A big man with big hands. A strong man. And he battered those girls to death. A man full of anger. And power.

I look at the cards again, trying to picture each of the men represented in the paper and ink in my hands. I put aside six of them. They were looking for sisters or brothers long lost, siblings their age or older. Old men, not strong enough to have done what the killer did.

I look at the remaining cards and discard four more of them. I remember these men, none of them big or angry enough to have done that kind of damage to the girls or to have killed Frank with that machete.

"I have two cards left. I need to see photographs of these men."

"I'll call the station," Carrick says, "see if I can find their drivers' licenses."

I hear Carrick talking into his cellphone in the other room. "Ria," he calls from the living room, "what's your email address? I'll have him email the photos."

Sometimes I forget in this house what technology is available to me. I quickly write down my address on the back of one of the discarded index cards and hand it to Carrick. I turn to go back to the kitchen, but he grabs my hand and holds onto me.

"Don't go," he mouths. He lifts my palm to his face, while he waits for an answer. "Okay," he says to the phone, "that's great.

"We'll have the photos in ten minutes. Meanwhile," he pulls me into his arms, "I have something I need to do."

And he proceeds to kiss the living daylights out of me, chasing all thoughts of everything except his lips from my mind. *I'm here*, I think, *right where I want to be*.

"Come on, Ria—" he grins at me salaciously "—let's go upstairs."

I grin right back at him. "Yeah, and check the computer in my bedroom." I waggle my eyebrows and he laughs, the sound welcome.

I log in, he prints off the photos. "Neither of them have a current license," he says, "they must have moved out of state."

"Let me see them." I grab for the pages, but he stops me. "Wait," he says. "We'll do this in the kitchen."

CHAPTER 24

"Him," I say as soon as I touch the second photograph. "It's him." The jolt throws me into Carrick's arms.

"He's not on the Marathon list," Uncle Jim points out. I know he's questioning the list and not my certainty but I respond anyway.

"It's him," I insist. "He's the one."

"Okay," Carrick's calm voice agrees. "He's the one. Have you seen him around the job site?"

"Of course I have," I realize with surprise. "And I know why he's not on the list. He's changed his name. He's changed his name to Scott. Oh, my God, he's taken the name Marylou used when she came to see me. And the only way he could have got that was from her. And he's a plumber. That's why I don't see him very often. He's usually working two or three weeks opposite me."

"Damn."

Carrick grabs the Marathon list and turns to the final page. "Scott, Tony. He started work a week after you did. I wonder how many of your other jobs he's worked on?"

The deep-rooted anger in Carrick's voice makes me shiver. "He's been watching me. I thought my discomfort on job sites was because I was the odd man out, the token woman who didn't fit in, who nobody really liked. I bet it was him."

I want to rip up the index card, the sheet of paper with his photograph, the Marathon list, but I don't. Instead, I wait to see what Carrick, now in full cop-mode, is going to do.

He doesn't disappoint me. He's on the phone to the chief and he doesn't try and hide his conversation from us.

"There's DNA evidence, Chief. All we need is a warrant to get that from Tony Scott and we've got him. Have the lab check the twins' evidence against Frank's. I'll bet you dinner that it was the same guy.

"Thanks, Chief," he says and hangs up.

"Home?" I ask. "Can we go home now?"

He smiles down at me and says the word I've been waiting forever to hear him say. "Home."

THE NEXT MORNING CARRICK is gone before the sun, leaving me a note on the pillow.

He's gone, the note says. *Not in his apartment, not at work. I'll call later.*

I press my lips against the *love, Carrick* at the bottom of the page and try to stop myself from reaching for the phone. When I do break down, it's to call home, not Carrick.

I tell Mom the news, the lack of it, I mean, then tell her I'll be home all day and I'll let her know if I hear anything else.

It's the perfect day to clean house. I have no commitments, Carrick's return to look forward to, *and* it's raining. What else would I do? I put the Proclaimers on the CD player, turn the volume up as high as it will go. I add the vacuum to the noise mix.

Halfway through "My Old Friend the Blues" I feel a draft. Fatcat hates the sound of the vacuum so I'm guessing he's escaped out the cat door. He won't be long. It's always a toss-up which he hates more—the rain or the noise.

I dance through the living room along with Craig and Charlie, my out-of-tune rendition swallowed up by the roar of the vacuum and the volume of the stereo.

It's a good thing too, because Fatcat howls even more when I sing than he does when he sees me bring out the Hoover.

When I'm finished downstairs, I shut off both machines and head into the kitchen for a glass of water and to tell Fatcat it's safe to come back inside. But he's there, hunched into a tiny ball under the table, his fur standing straight up. The hair on my neck rises to join it.

The reflection in the glass-fronted cabinet isn't mine. I turn slowly.

"Tony? Tony Scott?"

I know his face now that I see him in person. I've seen it over the years, first on my porch when he was pretending to look for his mother, then on job sites. Sometimes his hair is dark, sometimes light. Sometimes he wears glasses, sometimes he has a beard.

Today he's the uber-Tony: cropped short blond hair, clean-shaven, eyes such a light blue that they have to be his natural color. And they give me the creeps.

He must have used different names over the years but because I've only ever seen him in passing, I don't know any of them except the one he's using now. I try it again.

"Tony?"

He smiles at me and holds up a machete, the perfect match to the one found beside Frank Morrison's body. I suspect now that he used one just like it to carve up the girls as well.

I know I should be scared, and I am, but I've spent so much of the past couple of weeks frightened to death that finally facing one of my fears—one that's not in my own head—is freeing enough that I don't scream. Or faint.

I back away until I'm against the fridge and then I wait. There's nothing else I can do, he's too big and too fast for me. It's late in the afternoon and Carrick might show up at any time.

But, in the end, Carrick shows up too late. Tony comes farther into the kitchen, machete in hand, passing just a little too close to the table.

Fatcat uncurls himself and launches himself right at Tony's left arm, the one holding the machete. The weapon drops to the floor and Fatcat howls, scratching and climbing up Tony's arm. He reaches his shoulder and digs in. Now Tony's screaming and thrashing but all I hear is Fatcat and the faint sound of a siren in the distance.

I hear a clatter and watch as the machete skitters across the floor toward me. I grab it, needing both hands to pick it up. It's heavy, unbalanced for my height and weight, but I don't care. I point it at Tony.

"Fatcat," I say, calmly, "stay right there." Calm isn't difficult now because the sirens are right outside my door.

Fatcat has attached himself to the side of Tony's neck and I watch, mesmerized, as he digs in deeper and blood drips onto my kitchen floor. Tony screams, batting at Fatcat. He doesn't budge.

"Don't touch my cat," I say, sticking the point of the machete against his throat. "Just don't."

My arms are shaking with the strain but I don't move, not until the cavalry races in through the kitchen door.

"Ria?" He's yelling, his voice harsh and deep. He's as scared as I am.

"I'm here." I reassure him with a shaky smile and drop the machete to the floor.

He waits while the men with him handcuff Scott and then pulls Fatcat away from Scott, leaving deep, angry scratches on his arms and neck. Fatcat crouches under the table and growls until they close the door behind them, their last words, "Jones? You're on leave, right? We'll be in touch."

"How did you know?" I ask, my arms tight around his waist.

"A patrol car spotted his truck and followed him."

He takes a deep breath and reaches under the table, grabbing Fatcat and nestling him against his chest. "You, cat, will be eating tuna every day."

I smile, again, at both my heroes.

IT ISN'T LONG, NOT REALLY, though it feels like forever before they convict Tony Scott for the murders of Marylou and Maryjean Messier and Frank Morrison.

Carrick and I do our best to keep each other distracted, keep each other focused on other things, but it doesn't work except occasionally, when we manage to take each other into that other world. Then, for those few moments, we manage to forget about the case going on without us.

Uncle Jim is our conduit to the police department, Carrick having decided to stay on leave, at least until we sell his house and move his furniture into mine. We're also talking about a long vacation, someplace warm and sunny where we don't know a single person, and where no one knows me.

I think I've learned something of my gift. I know more about how it works, how little I can control it, and I've accepted that. And every morning, I thank Mama Amata for being there when I've really needed her.

And Carrick, too, has accepted my gift. I'm not sure he'll ever be truly comfortable with it, but he can live with it and that's all that matters.

And Fatcat? He *loves* Carrick Jones. I still have scratches on the backs of my hands and my ankles, but Fatcat spends most of his time purring in Carrick's lap.

If I was a little smaller, that's exactly what I'd be doing as well.

* * * * *

*Be sure to return to NEXT in November for
more entertaining women's fiction about
the next passion in a woman's life.
For a sneak preview of Peggy Webb's*
THE SECRET GODDESS CODE,
*coming to NEXT in November,
please turn the page.*

CHAPTER 1

"Where's the applause meter when you need it?"
—Gloria

I have died and gone to Mooreville, Mississippi.

I knew things were bad when that peroxided, collagen-enhanced, nubile nymph stole my role as the reigning TV goddess in "Love in the Fast Lane," but I didn't know I'd be killed off for real and sent to the backside of nowhere. Good lord, just because a woman turns forty-five shouldn't mean she gets tossed out and consigned to life without long-stemmed roses and Godiva chocolates.

Trying to make sense of things, I close my eyes, but when I open them again I'm staring at the same wide expanse of cloudy sky slashed with a sign that says *Welcome to Mooreville*. Plus, I have a lump on my head the size of California.

"Is anybody here?"

Expecting Saint Peter to answer, I ease up on my elbow and spot my powder blue Ferrari Spyder. Or what remains of it. They don't let you take cars to the hereafter, no matter which way you go, so this means I'm not dead.

To some people that would come as a relief, but the mood I'm in, it just makes me mad.

It also makes me remember swerving to miss a cow, then clawing my way out of the airbag in an adrenaline-propelled panic, which explains why I'm in a ditch.

When I left Hollywood and headed to my child-hood home in Jackson without even telling my agent, I expected headlines to read, "Famous Soap Opera Actress Disappears." Instead I've wrecked my car, maimed my cell phone and crippled myself, and there's not a single reporter around to turn this drama to my advantage. The situation calls for a major pity party.

I try to work up a few tears, but all I can see is how ludicrous my situation is: done in by a cow and my crazy urge to drive Mississippi's back roads. I start laughing and can't stop.

Somebody get the net. I've gone completely crazy and sirens signal the men in white are coming to take me away.

"Are you all right?"

Oh, my lord. A drop-dead handsome man in a fireman's uniform is talking to me. Either I bumped my head harder than I thought and am hallucinating, or Mooreville just started looking a whole lot better.

"That depends on how you describe all right."

The hunk kneels over me and pops the blood pressure cuff on while an older fireman and a paunchy state trooper scurry around my mutilated car.

"I'm Rick Miller, ma'am, and we're going to get you to the hospital over in Tupelo."

Now that made me mad. "I'm not old enough to be called ma'am, even in Mississippi."

The hunk, who is now checking me for broken bones, is wearing a wedding ring. Now maybe I *will* cry.

Not that I'm looking for a husband or anything remotely resembling one. But when a big chunk of your life gets ripped away and you don't have another person in this whole world to turn to, suddenly it feels as if you have nothing at all, that you're teetering on the edge of a cliff in the middle of a deserted jungle screaming for a net, and there's not even a slim chance anybody will hear.

"Listen, Rick, forgive me for being so flippant. It's not every day I run into a light pole. I don't know what I'm going to do about my poor car."

"I'll call Tuck's Tow service. Jackson Tucker's the best mechanic in this area." He wraps his fireman's jacket around me, then he and the other fireman lift me onto a gurney. "Is there anybody else you want me to call?"

"No," I say.

Shouldn't women my age have at least ten best friends on tap for situations like this? Both my parents are dead and nobody in Jackson was expecting me. "There's no one."

"Don't you worry, ma...uh..."

"Gloria. Gloria Hart."

"Miss Hart, I'll be right there with you."

My lord, I'd forgotten how sweet Southern hospitality can be.

I wonder what else I've forgotten. I've been caught up for so long in the world of daytime television drama, I don't know the first thing about the real world.

Cut from the soap opera that made her a star, America's TV goddess Gloria Hart heads back to her childhood home to regroup. But when a car crash maroons her in small-town Mississippi, it's local housewife Jenny Miller to the rescue. Soon these two very different women, together with Gloria's sassy assistant, become fast friends, realizing that they bring out a certain secret something in each other that men find irresistible!

Look for

THE SECRET GODDESS CODE

by

PEGGY WEBB

Available November wherever you buy books.

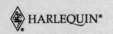

EVERLASTING LOVE™

Every great love has a story to tell™

Charlie fell in love with Rose Kaufman
before he even met her, through stories her
husband, Joe, used to tell. When Joe is killed
in the trenches, Charlie helps Rose through
her grief and they make a new life together.
But for Charlie, a question remains—can
love be as true the second time around?
Only one woman can answer that....

Look for

The Soldier and the Rose

by
Linda Barrett

Available November wherever you buy books.

REQUEST YOUR FREE BOOKS!

2 FREE NOVELS PLUS 2 FREE GIFTS!

There's the life you planned. And there's what comes next.

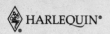

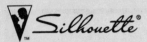

Romantic
SUSPENSE

**Sparked by Danger,
Fueled by Passion.**

Onyxx agent Sully Paxton's only chance of
survival lies in the hands of his enemy's daughter
Melita Krizova. He doesn't know he's a pawn in the
beautiful island girl's own plan for escape. Can
they survive their ruses and their fiery attraction?

*Look for the next installment in the
Spy Games miniseries,*

Sleeping with Danger

by **Wendy Rosnau**

Available November 2007 wherever you buy books.

HARLEQUIN *Romance*

New York Times bestselling author

DIANA PALMER

Handsome, eligible ranch owner Stuart York knew Ivy Conley was too young for him, so he closed his heart to her and sent her away—despite the fireworks between them. Now, years later, Ivy is determined not to be treated like a little girl anymore…but for some reason, Stuart is always fighting her battles for her. And safe in Stuart's arms makes Ivy feel like a woman…his woman.

Winter Roses

Available November.

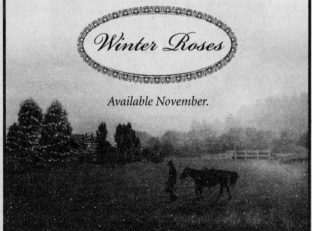